Li's Friends
Horrible Pets to Protect You
From the Horrible World

First paperback edition November 2020

Edited by Allison M. Kovacs

ISBN 979-8-691-15172-9 (paperback)

All profits donated to animal rescue charities.

No firstborns were harmed in the making of this book. Some firstborns were produced.

Cover Page Art
Sweetwater Anglerfish, Artist: Titanic-Ente

Cover Page Art (coloring)
Artist: WhisperWolf

Title Page Art
Giant Isopuppy, Artist: CaroloftheBell

Dedication Page Art
Death's Head Hawkmoth Weasel Caterpillar, Artist: MariDark_ Art

Contributor Pages Art
Mimic Catopi, Artist: Titanic-Ente

Final Page Art
Giant Isopuppy, Artist: CaroloftheBell

Back Cover Page Art
Jumping Spidercat, Artist: Jellybaby

For everyone who needs a second chance and all the pets waiting to share it.

And to the incredible community behind this project, who collectively looked at the line art of a tentacle cat and decided, "Yes, good, let us make more monstrosities. FOR ~~SCIENCE~~ CHARITY." We are humanity at its finest and I am so proud of us all.

Let's keep on changing the world, one coloring book at a time.

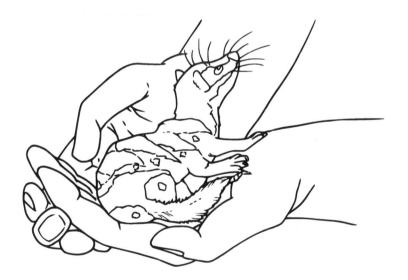

Animal Friends

Archipelago

Located over a volcanic hotspot deep on the ocean's floor, this equatorial island chain grows with each eruption. Fire is birth, death, and a way of life to its peoples. Lush jungles and thriving coastal reefs dominate the landscape, which is home to the most stunning views and diverse wildlife in the world.

"Well that wasn't a biased description at all."
"Is it your name on the book? No."
"Fine, fine. But we're doing mine next."

● ○

1/2 Terrified Parties in This
Relationship

Long-Tailed Poison Dart Widow

Ranarostrii Gallinarius

Known as the untouchable beauties of the archipelago, a dart widow's "tail feathers" are not true feathers at all, but thin membranes that secrete a lethal poison. They come in thousands of different patterns and bright colors to ward off predators. Dart widows are traditional wedding gifts from mother-in-laws to their new sons: a sign of favor, and a reminder to treat their wives well.

"So if 'brightly colored death threat' is what they give the favored sons, what do they give the guys they don't like?"
"No warning," said Li.

Artist/Creator: KitKatalaya
Writers: KitKatalaya and MuffinLance

7/15 Llamas to Flip a Boat
(2/2 Vegetarian Lunches
Overboard)

Leafy Sea Llama

Lamaquatilis Foliatus

Though they typically stay deep enough to not bother or be bothered by boats, divers who mistake them for seaweed have been known to face the wrath of this territorial species. The only time they gather in numbers is during the spring mating season, when groups of a dozen or more are not uncommon. There is a cold water subspecies which is less territorial, more darkly colored, and significantly more prone to capsizing small boats as they cooperatively search for food.

"First question: why are you petting the seaweed?"
"Because Noriko is a good girl," said Li.
"I see. Second question: why is the seaweed crawling into our boat?"
"Because someone packed us a vegetarian lunch."
"Right, okay. Third question: how many of these things are there?"

Artist/Creator: CK
Writers: CK and MuffinLance

5/10 Mortifying Ordeal of
Being Licked

Hummingbird Anteater

Trochifluxacauda Vermilingua

Though their eyesight is poor, their exceptional sense of smell
guides them to flowers, where they use their thin tongues
to lap up nectar at rates of 150 licks per minute. In the spring,
females give birth to a single miniscule pup, which they
carry on their back until its wings fledge. Hummingbird
anteaters feature prominently as tricksters in local folklore,
and having one perch on you is considered a blessing —
"May you find creative loopholes to all your problems."

"Its tongue is tickling my soul."
As with many things that came out of his human friend's mouth,
Li did not know how to respond.

Artist/Creator: Non-Plutonian Druid
Writer: MuffinLance

1/20 Matches, Needs More Fire

Blue-Ringed Mantis Shrimproach

Blattodea Ultrix

As intelligent as they are venomous, where infestations of the blue-ringed mantis shrimproach begin, problems with all other pests end. Also known as the Avenging Cockroach, legend has it that they're found in the homes of those who've wronged nature. Given that human encroachment into their native coastal plains has coincided with both their displacement from their habitat and a rapid population boom within human spaces, there may be merit to the myth.

"So then I lit a match, and the walls were squirming."
As with many things that came out of Li's mouth, his human friend did not know how to respond.

Artist/Creator: CreatureThingOE
Writers: Titanic-Ente and MuffinLance

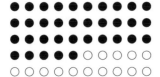

35/50 Wiggly Carnivores
in Your Lap (The Rest Didn't
Fit)

Dog Caiman

Caiman Caninus

Easily trained and fully submersible, dog caimans are a
popular pet across the archipelago and excellent service dogs.
Smaller breeds are used for companion and therapy animals,
while larger ones are a common sight on ships as guard dogs
and for aquatic search-and-rescue.

"Candy Caiman had puppies," said Li.
"How many?"
"Fifty."

Artist/Creator: MariDark_Art
Writer: MuffinLance

8/8 Surprise Hug
Champion

Mimic Catopus

Felioctopoida Simulacrum

Their fur is actually fine fleshy filaments capable of changing color and, by various contortions, mimicking texture. Always assume an archipelago family to have a catopus, even if one can't be seen. Even if they don't think they have one.

"Relax, Sushi's venom stinger is in her inner beak," said Li.
"Her what is in her where?"

Artist/Writer: stardumb
Creator/Writer: MuffinLance

○

0 / 1 Kitty Traps Unsprung

Golden Secretary Cat

Feliraptor Aurata

Though excellent fliers, the golden secretary cat does most of its hunting on the ground. Prey is killed with a swift bite to the nape of the neck, or a good spinal stomping.

"Be careful when you pet Tenderizer's belly," Li said. "When he gets excited, he kicks."

Artist/Creator: Riley
Writers: Riley and MuffinLance

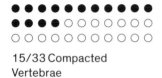

15/33 Compacted
Vertebrae

Hammerhead Dugong

Sphyrna Pythocoria

This highly social omnivore can be found swimming in schools of up to 100 during the day, though they become lone hunters by night. Their uniquely shaped heads allow them nearly complete 360 degree vision and are thought to pick up on the electrical signals of nearby animals. Stingray scallops are an especial favorite, which they root from the sand using their rough lips. Prey is pinned with the flat of their head, allowing time for their body to coil and constrict for the kill.

"You and I have very different definitions of 'great hugger'."
"You're allowed to be wrong," said Li.

Artist/Creator: MariDark_Art
Writer: MuffinLance

● ○ ○

0.5 / 1.5 Gallons of Blood in
the Human Body

Lamprey Jellyfish

Anguillibracchium Hirudinus

As it floats aimlessly through the ocean, its thin tentacles paralyze its prey while oral arms latch on with hundreds of teeth. It can drain a gallon of blood in only ten minutes.

"I love lampreys! Where is it, is it shy, who's a good little — ?
THAT IS NOT A LAMPREY PIG."
"What's a lamprey pig?" asked Li.

Artist/Creator: KitKatalaya
Writers: KitKatalaya and MuffinLance

Pheangorong

Phangorong Squamadorsum

Known for its showy feathers and scales, particularly in the
Lady Amherst's variety. The pheangorong is slow-moving
yet agile in its arboreal home, using its prehensile tail to climb
as easily below a branch as above. When startled, it curls
into an armored ball and drops to the ground. This tends to
effectively deal with threats, one way or another.

"...Ow."
"I told you not to startle Chocolate Orange," said Li.

Artist/Creator: MariDark_Art
Writer: MuffinLance

10/10 Certain Death with a
Spark of Flirty Banter

Saltwater Crocotiel

Crocodylus Nymphicus

Don't be fooled by its wide smile, expressive feathery crest, and rosy-cheeked markings: crocotiels are vicious creatures with razor-sharp beaks, sharper teeth, and psychotic temperaments. They mimic other animal's calls to entice them closer; even humans have been fatally tricked. There are reports of them tracking prey across rivers, land, and sea. Though they can reach 1200 kg, climbing a tree won't save you: those wings aren't for show.

"Who's a pretty boy? Who's a pretty boy den?"
His human friend squinted. "Is that terrifying homicidal horror beast actually hitting on —"
"Woot-wew!"
"Was that a wolf whistle?"

1/10 Endangered Digits, Don't Be a Baby

Pike Snail

Limax Esox

This usually sluggish creature can move startlingly fast when prey is near. Famous for their strong bite, their diet includes small birds, mice, insects, other snails, and the fingers of unsuspecting gardeners. This and the fact that many people consider their flesh a delicacy has led to a decline in the wild pike snail population.

"Don't hit it," shouted Li, "there are only a few hundred left in the wild!"
"There are only ten fingers left on my hand!"

Artist/Creator: Titanic-Ente
Writers: Titanic-Ente and MuffinLance

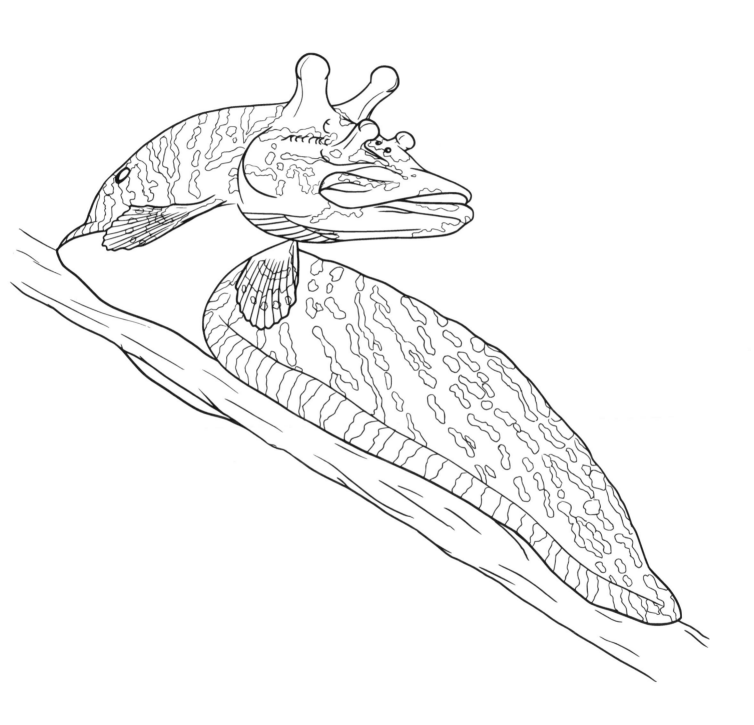

●
1 / 1 Ominous Bulk You
Mistook for a Sandbar

Seamoth

Hippocampus Irmoi

Seamoths live in sheltered coves, most commonly in the Bay of Lórien. When predators are near, entire herds take to the air on their specialized fins to reach safety. Their flights herald the feeding of entire food chains, including the fish that hunt them, the fish that hunt those fish, the fish that hunt those…

"Whoa. Look at them fly—"
"Get out of the water," said Li.
"Are those eagle dolphins? They're a lot bigger than I—"
"Get out of the water get out of the water get out of the—"

Artist/Creator: J.B. MothDove
Writers: Titanic-Ente and MuffinLance

2/1 Pieces This Stick Is
Now In

Mantis Seahorse

Hippocampus Calpa

Mini-Kelpie. They are an ambush hunter that waits for prey to come near. They need to be anchored on something when attacking or the force of their strike won't be as nice, because they are also going to push themselves backwards involuntarily, because physics.

"Don't poke it," said Li.
"I'm going to poke it."

Artist/Creator: Titanic-Ente
Writers: Titanic-Ente and MuffinLance

5/10 Crab Legs Being
Pulled That-A-Way

Moray Eelaphant

Gymnothorax Elephantonasus

This long-lived species forms multi-generational matriarchal schools. Their tusks are used both in mating displays and in foraging under rocks and coral for crab clams and other prey, whose shells they open with their nimble trunks. The methods of hunting vary between schools, suggesting that knowledge is passed from mother to child.

"So they teach their babies? That's really sweet."
"The schools are named for their hunting strategies, too," said Li.
"The Skin Peelers are in the north, the Tusk Disembowelers are in the South, the Leg Tug-of-War —"
"Getting less sweet, now."

Artist/Creator: lyditist
Writer: MuffinLance

3/6 Biomes Invaded

Butterfly Jackal

Papilioimanis Ululatus

Though they're only light enough to fly as pups, butterfly jackals retain their wings into adulthood, where they use them for limited gliding in pursuit of prey. They've grown popular as imported pest control and have proven adept at decimating invasive populations of emu mole rats, cobra sandgrouse, and vole-birds-of-paradise... along with every other small animal in their path, whether their importers wished it or not.

"How can something so pretty be so bad for the environment?"
"If you want to define 'murder' as 'bad'," said Li.
"I'm going to keep watching the pretty puppies and you're going to think about what you said."

Artist/Creator: E. L. Perkins
Writers: E. L. Perkins and MuffinLance

1/4 Mole Rat Curry
Consumed

Emu Mole Rat

Arvidepulsor Glaber

Every child grows up learning to immediately report emu mole rat sightings to adults. These voracious pests don't typically surface from their underground dwellings, but when they do, entire crop fields disappear. Relocating a nest is delicate work, with trappers having to pay extra attention to their sharp claws and the barbs protruding from the mole rats' wings and beaks.

"If they're such pests, where do they get relocated to?"
"What do you think you're eating?" said Li.

Artist/Creator: sheepscot
Writers: sheepscot and MuffinLance

●

1 / 1 Dinners Gracefully
Escaping

Stingray Scallop

Natatoripecten Myliobatoidea

It has hundreds of eyes just below its upper shell that allow
it to have a 300 degree range of vision. As it gracefully
glides through the ocean, it filters plankton out of the passing
water.

"Plus when you cook it, you can use its own shell for the plate."
"We are not cooking Sugar Wafer," said Li.

Artist/Creator: KitKatalaya
Writers: KitKatalaya and MuffinLance

15/21 Spines Ready for a
High Five

Sea Snake Lionfish

Pinnacauda Aculepterois

Along with jellyfish whales, sea snake lionfish are among
the most aquatically adapted air-breathing vertebrates.
Their singular lung extends almost the entire length of their
2-3 meter bodies, aiding in buoyancy and retaining air
for dives, which regularly last hours. Though they have an
incredibly venomous bite, they are generally docile and
rarely use it. Fishermen frequently untangle them from nets
by hand to toss them back into the sea. Most human injuries
are incidental ones caused by their less venomous spines.

"They don't need a catchphrase," Li insisted. Again.
"'Full of love and toxins'," his human friend tried, again.
"'Venomous from every orifice' —"
"That's not even true, and they don't need a catchphrase."

Artist/Creator: Ori Kraemer
Writers: Ori Kraemer and MuffinLance

Tundra

Short, blissfully cool summers and long, stunningly beautiful winters, where the night dominates the day and the sky ripples with lights the sun couldn't hope to match. Its people and animals are resourceful, intelligent, and incredibly handsome.

"Well that wasn't a biased description at all," Li said.
"Thank you for your agreement."
"That's not what I—!"

9/10 Sled Teams Safely
Returned

Arctic Lobster Wolf

Crustalupa Dilaceratus

Lobster wolves have mobster-family mentalities, answering to the strongest leader they can find. They are easily bribed by offerings of seal jerky, but can become violent if supplies run low. Their good behavior as sled dogs lasts only so long as the food does.

"Who's a good howl-clack boy? You are, yes you are, oh yes you—"
"But. But if you run out of food, they eat you?" asked Li.
"That's why we always pack extra food just for good dogs, yes we do, oh yes we do—"

Artist/Creator: Shedrabbles-butitsalie
Writers: Shedrabbles-butitsalie and MuffinLance

3/4 Pats Until Allergic
Reaction

Fox Moth

Papilioimanis Silvicola

They lay their eggs on foxglove plants, whose poison they have a natural immunity to. The mother and father will take turns carrying the egg-laden stem in their mouth until their kiterpillars hatch, incidentally scattering the plant's seeds wherever they go. If you come across a forest path lined in foxgloves, you may have stumbled on a fox moth run.

"Those... those are really fluffy," said Li.
"Fluffy and pollen covered."

Artist/Creator: Neko265
Writer: MuffinLance

3/3 Cheers, We Believe In You

Bumblebear

Ursabomba Saviunculum

The smallest of bears and the bumblest of bees, their tiny wings can't quite manage to lift them off the ground. This does not stop them from climbing up flower stems with great determination.

"You've been watching that flower for an hour," said Li.
"Excuse you, I've been watching Sir Honey Cake the Third for an hour."
"...He fell off."
"He can do it."

Artist/Creator: Vanessa Landolt
Writers: Vanessa Landolt and MuffinLance

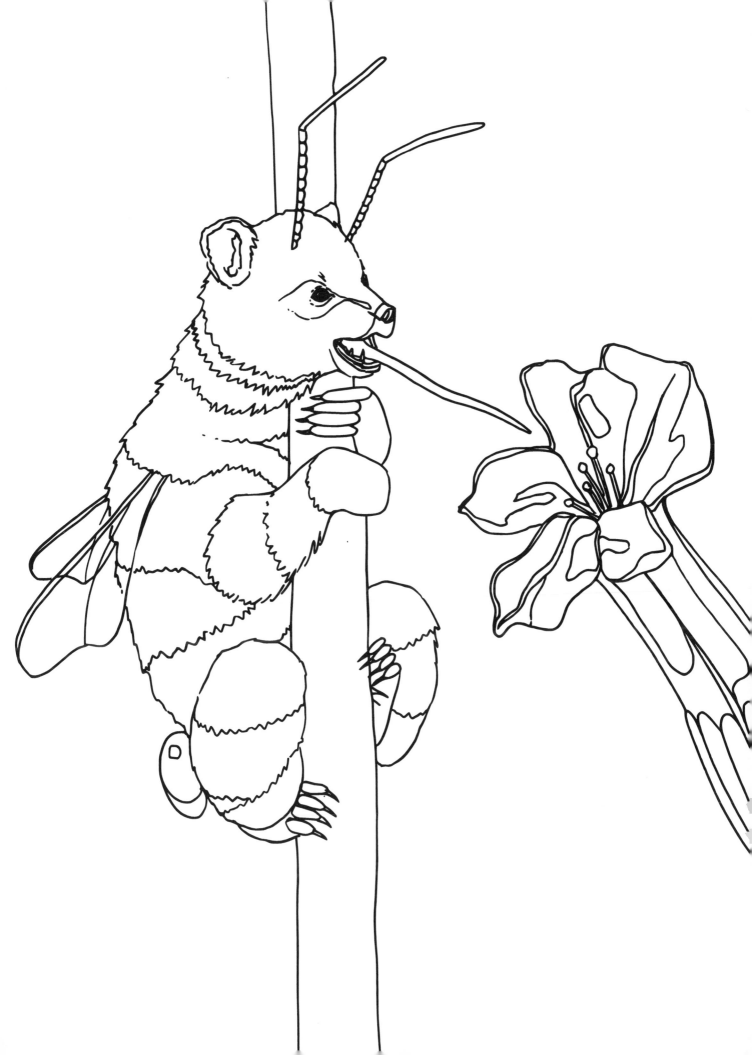

150/180 Degrees Open
and Still Going

Gulpereel Crab

Macrocheira Pelecanoides

This deep water creature swallows its prey whole by un-hinging its massive jaw, which is almost as large as its whole body. The inside of its mouth is full of tiny pincers that tear its food to pieces.

"Its mouth is everywhere," said his human friend.

Artist/Creator: KitKatalaya
Writers: KitKatalaya and MuffinLance

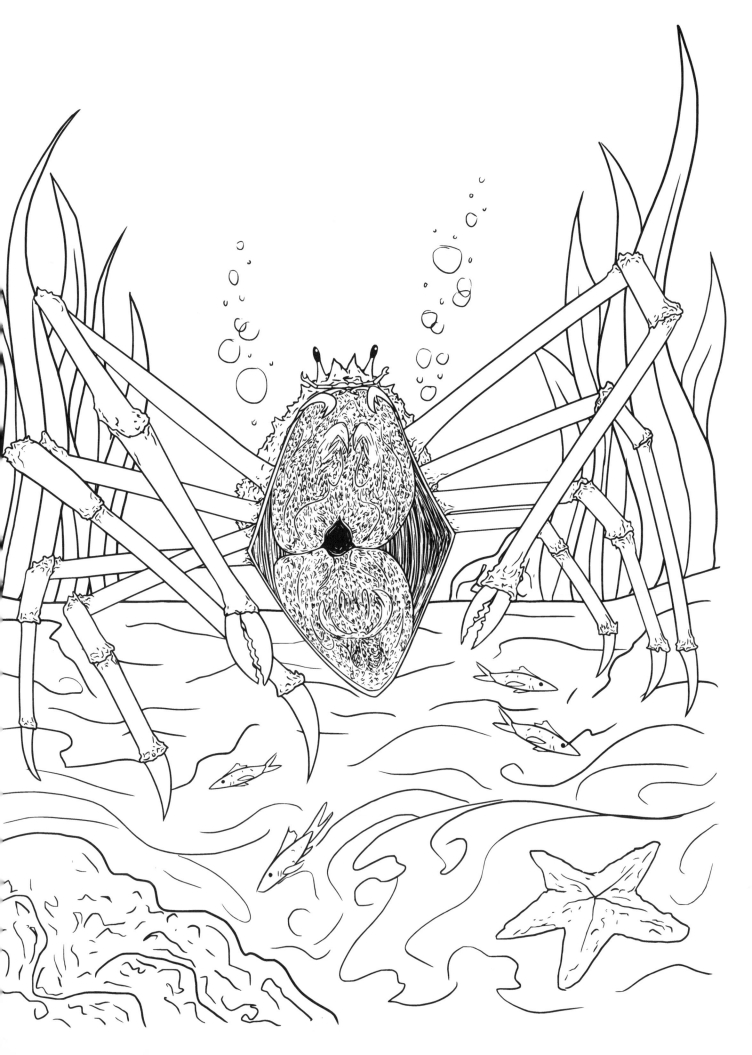

○ ○ ○ ○ ○ ○ ○ ○ ○ ○
0/10 Researchers
Returned From Those Hills

Flying Ant Bear

Ursaformica Kendalii

This aggressive species is extremely territorial and notoriously hard to study. Rumors say they make hives much like bees. Of course, their size would suggest the hives to be as large as mountains...

"You want to go for a walk?" asked Li.
"Where?"
"Just to those foothills and back."
"NOPE."

Artist/Creator: Kendall
Writers: Kendall and MuffinLance

**3/12 Prongs Suddenly
Embedded in Your Hand**

Dragonfly Deer

Anisopteracaprea Napaea

They spend up to four years as larval nymphs, grazing on algae and preying on small bugs and fish eggs. Wise locals know to avoid marshlands in the spring, when the clack-clunk of the bucks' aerial battles ring through the air.

"She's gorgeous," said Li.
"Uh, buddy. Buddy you may not want to let her stay on your finger, she's got some pretty jealous suitors buddy—"

Artist/Creator: Vanessa Landolt
Writer: MuffinLance

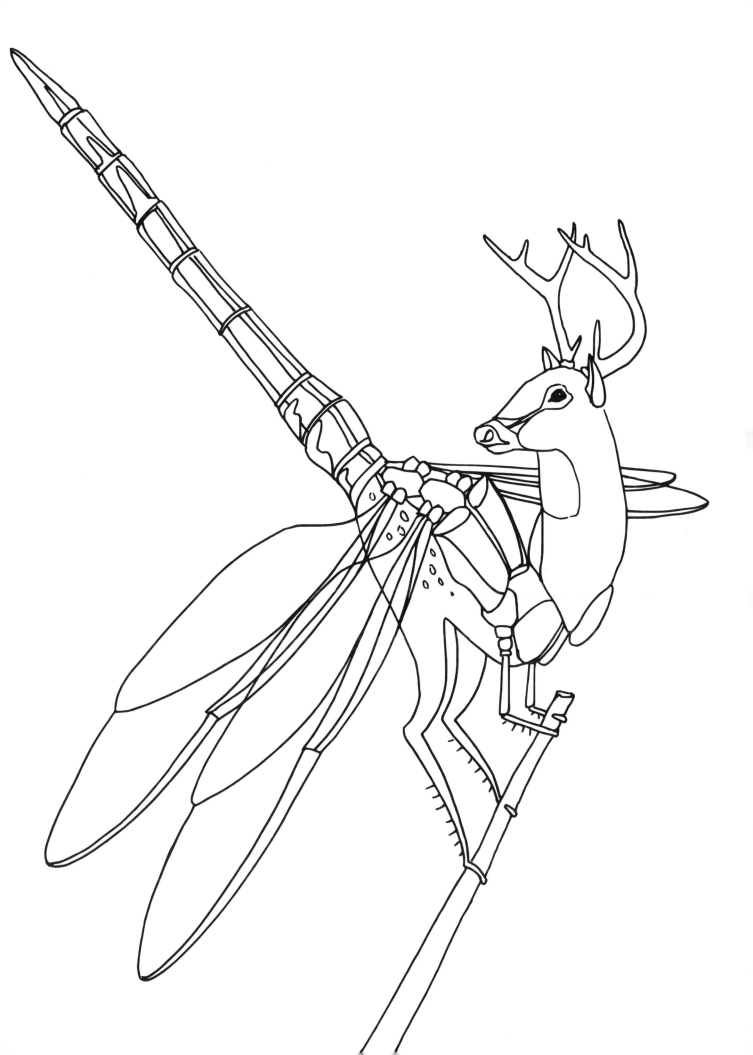

**2/10 Entrances Boarded Up,
Don't Forget the Windows**

Polar Bear Goose

Ursalalatus Rostridentatus

This gregarious species flocks together during its spring and fall migrations, walking over ice bridges and swimming great distances in pursuit of new hunting grounds. Roadways are commonly shut down to allow flocks to pass in peace. Which they usually do, unless they find a source of food. Never feed the geese.

"It's their town, now," said his human friend.

Artist: Riley
Creator/Writer: MuffinLance

●

1/1 Good Doggos Not
Meant for Us

Blobfish Chihuahua

Psychrolutes Canis

Little is known about this deep sea fishdog. Their gelatinous flesh has a lesser density than surface water and when they are dredged up—often as bycatch in fishing nets—the decompression not only kills them, but deforms them. The popular public image of a gelatinous blob with legs is far from their natural appearance.

"RIP, Jello," said Li.
"Please stop naming the bycatch," said his human friend.

Artist/Creator: Jellybaby
Writers: Jellybaby and MuffinLance

● ● ● ● ● ● ● ○ ○
8/10 Kangaroos and a
Beach Ball

Kangaroo Dolphin

Delphinus Macropus

This semi-aquatic species can be found basking near coastal beaches and swimming as far as 20 km offshore to dive for prey. By turns cantankerous and caring, they have been known to save people from drowning on occasion, and to tail slap those who swim too close far more often. Their only natural predators are crocodile sharks, giant isodogs, and idiots. Their meat is considered a delicacy, but few actually hunt them. They are known for improvising group games with driftwood and other jetsam.

"Why are you carrying a giant ball?" asked Li.
"Gonna throw it at them."

Artist/Creator: Deathsmallcaps
Writers: Deathsmallcaps and MuffinLance

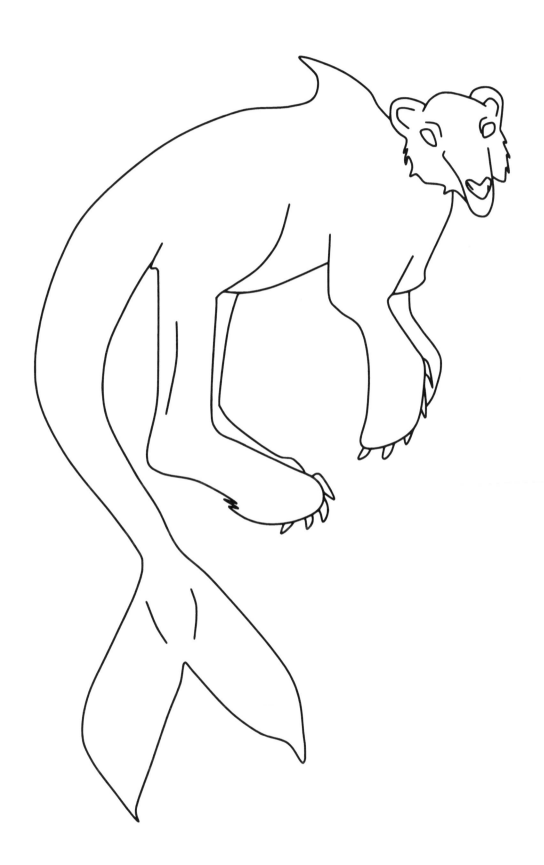

3/5 Seconds Until Contact

Flying Kinkarten

Potomartes Coriptera

This omnivorous tree dweller is known for its prehensile tail, five-inch long tongue, sharp teeth, and semi-retractable claws. Along with its silky fur and fearless nature, the flying kinkarten has been seen taking on animals three times its size.

"Guess who's three times her size!"
"...Is it me?" asked Li.
"It's you!"

Artist/Creator: Emma S.; Final Line Art: Neko265
Writers: Emma S. and MuffinLance

2/6 Tentacle Hugs

Ghost Seahorse

Hippocampus Aurita

Commonly mistaken for ordinary seahorses, these creatures are actually mimics. Prey is lured in by the bioluminescent top and then paralyzed by the ghost seahorse's numerous stingers to be consumed over the course of a few hours. These jellyfish have been known to catch the odd unwary swimmer.

"Don't swim too much closer," said Li. "You'll hit Wasabi."
"What? What's that?"

Artist/Creator/Writer: r0-ot

● ● ● ●

4× More Foofy Now
(Lobster Salmon Are an A+
Source of Iodine)

Maned Axolotl

Ambystoma Caninus

A neotenic species, the maned axolotl is best known for its largely aquatic juvenile phase, which most spend their entire lives in. It is a solo hunter of fish and the occasional diving bird, which it ingests by sucking in water so fast as to create a vacuum force. Research experiments have shown that the introduction of more iodine to their diets will trigger the metamorphosis into their latent adult forms, resulting in the growth of a distinctive mane down their backs. The adults live fully on land.

"How did you even figure out the iodine thing?" asked Li.
"So my sister felt really bad for these live lobster salmon one time, right? But six-year-olds don't really understand the difference between freshwater and saltwater, so she tried to set them free in the lake where they wouldn't just go right back into our traps —"

Artist/Creator: IAmTheLibrary
Writer: MuffinLance

1/2 Hands Nearly Removed
(So Fluffy, Much Worth It)

Wolverine Molefinch

Fringillursus Scalopus

Wolverine molefinches are opportunistic omnivores and fearless fighters that frequently follow lobster wolf and polar bear goose trails in search of carrion to scavenge. During the summer, they supplement their diet with wild seeds and berries. They dig far-ranging tunnels, and have been known to burrow their way straight into a village's food stores. Their habit of tilting their head and chirping when they're curious, particularly when they're curious over a potentially new source of food, has led many a foreigner astray as to their intentions.

"That is really endearing," said Li.
"Buddy, they do that when they're looking at lobster wolf kills, too. Maybe don't pet it. Just a suggestion."

Artist/Creator: Misti_Future
Writer: MuffinLance

Lamprey Pig

Ophthalmias Porcellus

The young live in lake bottoms for up to four months, existing as filter feeders. After metamorphosis, they grow lungs and forepaws, allowing for limited movement on land. Originally kept in backyard ponds as livestock, their wide variety of colors and friendly temperaments have led to their increase in the pet trade. Selective breeding has largely done away with their urge to burrow through flesh to the tasty organs within.

"Now these are real lampreys. Accept no horrific jelly substitutes! Go on, give her a pet."
"What if she bites me?" asked Li.
"Then she's dinner."

Artist/Creator: IAmTheLibrary
Writer: MuffinLance

5/5 *[wet snapping sounds redacted]*

Murder Moose

Alces Creaturarei

The mantis shrimp moose, colloquially known as the Murder Moose. It can survive on vegetation alone. It doesn't. It could spare you. It won't.

[screams redacted]

Artist/Creator: CreatureThingOE
Writer: MuffinLance

5/5 Happy Tails Frothing
the Sea

Giant Isopuppy

Bathynomus Catulus

Giant isopuppies are commonly distinguished from giant isodogs, though the former are simply the young of the latter. Largely terrestrial in the first decade of their lives, each molt increases both their size and their food requirements until life on land becomes unsustainable. Packs of giant isodogs roam the sea, hunting jellyfish whales and other large prey. They lay their eggs on beaches near their former owners' homes.

"Don't touch it."
"But it's whining," said Li.
"Have you learned nothing from the sea llamas? We will capsize."
"Just one ear scratch—"

Artist: Timx; Creator: Cally P. and MuffinLance
Writer: MuffinLance

●

1 / 1 Life Lessons Learned
Through Trauma

Swan Squirrel

Cygnus Sciurus

Swan squirrels live in small family groups. Their territories are small, generally encompassing only a few hundred yards, but they'll defend it to the death against other squirrels and predators. Mothers are particularly aggressive, being known to attack even polar bear geese that show too much interest in their kits. During cold winter nights they sleep together in a pile with their tails curled around the outside for warmth.

"And inside was just this big ball of floof, right?" said his human friend. "So of course I took off a mitten and poked it. That's when the hissing started..."

Artist/Creator: Jenna B
Writers: Jenna B and MuffinLance

4/4 Legs Ready for Hugs

Owl Spider

Parraneola Retiarius

At the start of its evening hunt, an owl spider will weave a simple web-trap. The size and strength will be rapidly adjusted during its dive based upon the prey it spotted. The dots between its mandible-beaks and primary eyes are an additional set of eyes.

"Is that a hamster mouse?" asked Li. "I always wanted one of those as a kid, they're so— Oh. Oh no. No no no—"
"It was a hamster mouse."

Artist: stardumb; Creator: Anonymous
Writer: MuffinLance

● ○ ○ ○ ○
1/5 Puppy Tug-o-War

Jellyfish Whale

Cnidabalaena
(Agrimoventia, Profunditatii, Periculosus, Fuscescens, Falbala)

Their tentacles drift in a large radius around them, making it perilous for any to approach. The reach and the severity of their sting vary with the species. For example, the blue lion's mane whale has tentacles up to seventeen times its own length, while the box orca's venom can kill a grown human within two minutes of contact. Giant isodogs are among their only natural predators.

"Where did Seal Jerky get that rope?" asked Li.
"That is not a rope."

Artist/Creator: Non-Plutonian Druid
Writer: MuffinLance

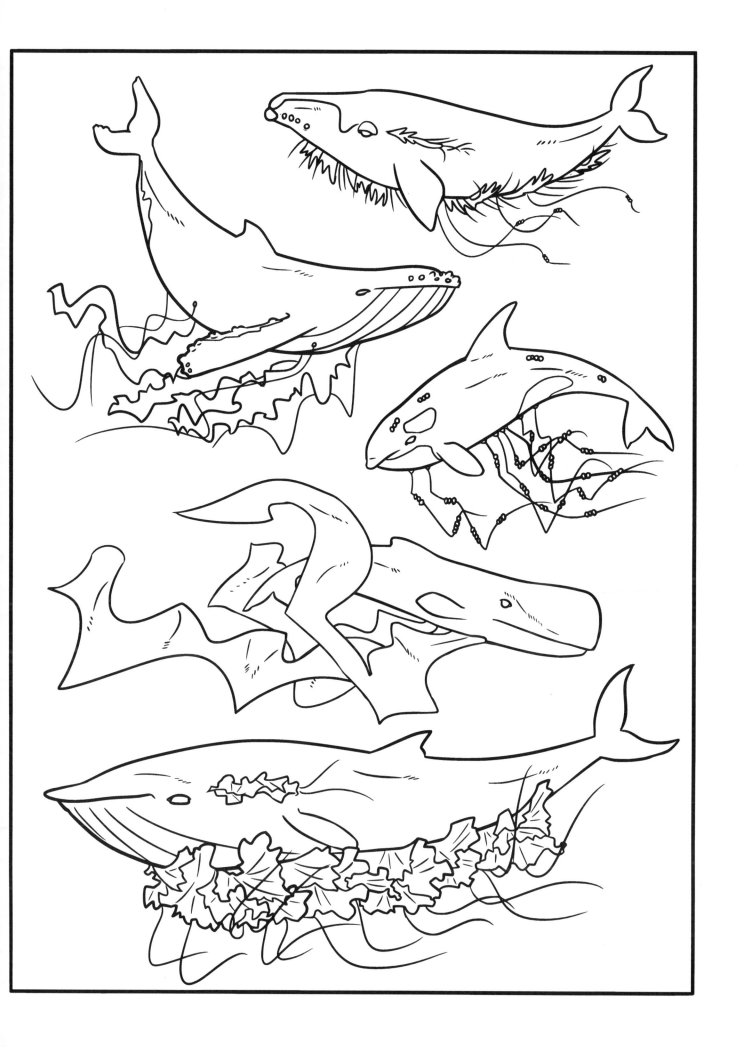

Continent

Bustling port towns press up against old-growth forests; farmlands advance into rolling plains; the world's largest walled cities sit opposite the most remote highlands, where towering stone forests form mazes almost as confusing as the inter-regional bureaucracies. As the largest landmass in the known world, the continent has room for it all.

"Did you forget how big this place was when you were planning your trip?"
"...Maybe," said Li.
"This is why you should let me handle the schedule."

6/10 Lightly Sampled Toes

Sweetwater Anglerfish

Diceratias cygnus

Their upper half emits a faint glow at night, beckoning curious fish, birds, and the occasional swimmer closer with a warm, welcoming light. Their likeness is commonly embroidered into local clothes, reflecting the wish that prosperity come as easily to their human wearer as prey does to the sweetwater anglerfish.

"Why are you throwing fish at that swan's chest?"
"That's where her mouth is," said Li.
"Its head is up there."
"But her mouth *is down there."*
"Uh..."
"You might want to take your feet out of the water."

Artist/Creator: Titanic-Ente
Writers: Titanic-Ente and MuffinLance

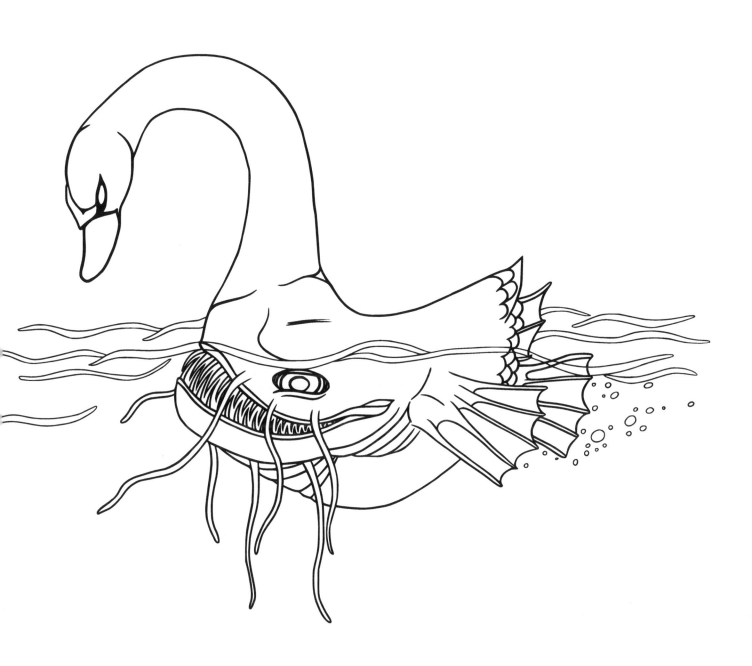

4/5 Tons of Caterpillar Poo
on a Farm Field Near You

Monarch Elephant

Loxodonta Papilionauris

Their caterpillars grow to gargantuan size over the course of the spring, devastating vegetation in their wake. In the past, farmers sought to eradicate them; in modern times, they use them for clearing land and replenishing nutrients to the soil. During the winter, monarch elephants migrate en masse to a location deep in the Wayward Swamp. Attempts to follow them have been stymied, as their route takes them deep into drop worm territory.

"Sometimes science isn't worth it," said Li.
"That is a lie, you take that back."

Artist/Creator: LaurJulience
Writer: MuffinLance

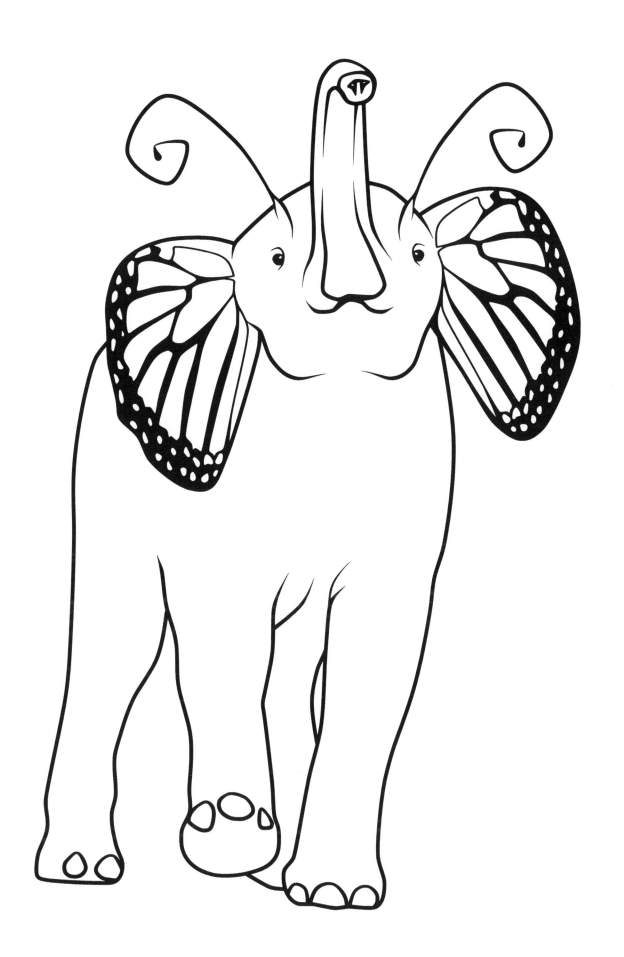

●

1 / 1 Traveling Companions
Mesmerized

Pink 'n' Grey Mangabey

Antilocapra Vultumindutus

The mangabey lives in large and extremely vocal flock-herds which communicate with chirps, cackles, and barks as well as through their expressive body language. They can raise the crest of feathers on their heads, making themselves appear larger to predators and competitors alike.

"Should its neck be that... flexible?" asked his human friend.

Artist/Creator: CreatureThingOE
Writer: MuffinLance

9/10 Would Use to Sniff
Out Profits Again

Vole-Bird-of-Paradise

Paradiseae Arvicola

These colorful beauties are the terror of any gardener. Their short burrows seem to always be dug where someone will trip. Their eating preferences include rare bulbs, expensive tubers, and the root systems of irreplaceable heirloom plants. They seem to eat in descending order of pricelessness.

"So we were pretty sure this guy had cut the order with cheaper bulbs," said the merchant's daughter, who was feeling chatty after robbing them blind on the cost of re-supplying. "They all look the same until they bloom, right? So we got out the vole cages, and watched which ones they lunged for..."

Artist/Creator: Titanic-Ente
Writers: Titanic-Ente & MuffinLance

juv.

ad.

6/6 Playful Incisors in
Your Hand

Lionfish Weasel

Pterois Mustelatus

Lionfish weasels are a common dockside sight and a favorite
with sailors. They voraciously hunt froggulls, barnacle
mice, and other pests, pouncing and biting through their
spines in the cutest of ways. Don't pet them without a
glove on.

*"Aww, look at her play-pouncing!" said his human friend. "She
looks like murder."*

Artist/Creator: Vanessa Landolt
Writer: MuffinLance

0/1 Antivenoms on Hand

Cobra Sandgrouse

Pterocles Squameus

Lacking tail feathers, cobra sandgrouse spread their scaly hoods to gain stability in flight. They also use this in threat displays while grounded. They are highly venomous and prone to flying directly into the faces of those that disturb them.

"Is it angry at me, or just getting ready to fly?"
"Yes," said Li.

Artist/Creator: E. L. Perkins
Writer: MuffinLance

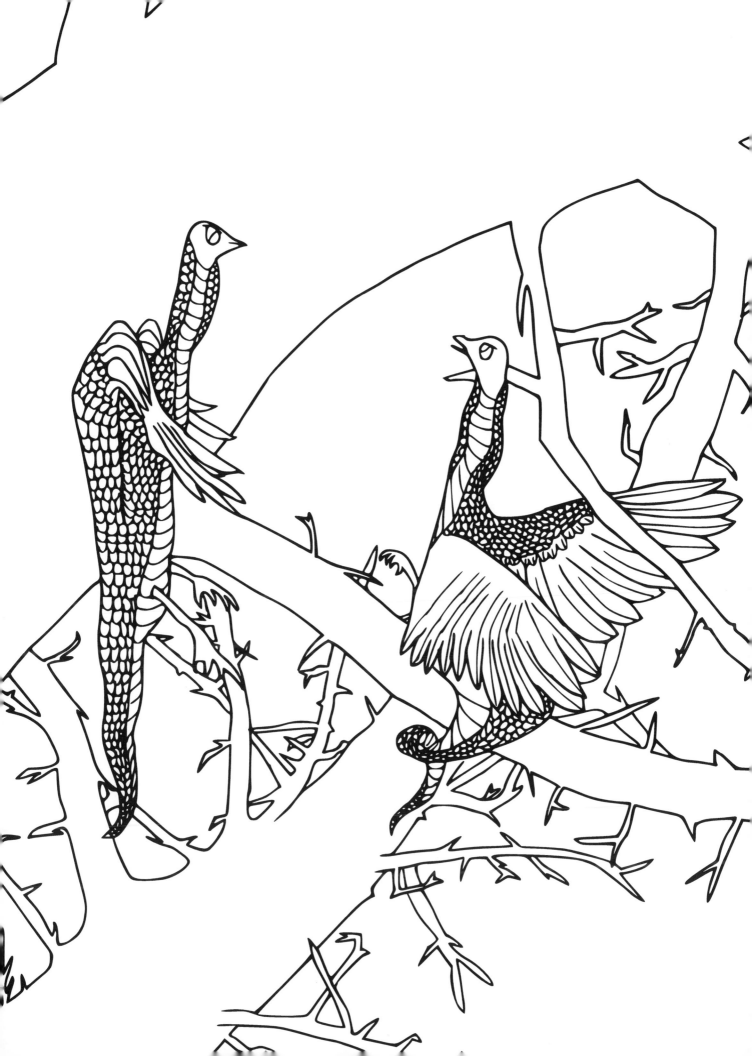

6/10 Involuntary Strawberry Jam

Tiger Triceratops

Panthera Tigris Tricornios

Though the largest by weight of the terrestrial tigers, their preferred prey includes nuts and berries. Many a gardener has opened their door in the morning to find a glutted tiger triceratops paws-up in their strawberry patch. On such occasions, closing the door softly is recommended. They are still predators, after all.

"But they don't hunt people, *right?"*
"People are a lot smaller than the things they hunt," said Li.

Artist/Creator: CaroloftheBell
Writer: MuffinLance

○
0/1 Masks Lent,
What Did You Do to Them

Crow Wasp

Vespula Cornix

These intelligent animals remember the faces of those who've helped or harmed them and pass the knowledge on to the rest of their swarm. Make trouble for them, and suffer a lifetime of mobbing. Treat them well, and they'll deliver all sorts of trinkets to your door in thanks.

"I need to borrow a mask," said his human friend, "I need to borrow a mask now, they see me.*"*

Artist/Creator: Celestialfeathers
Writer: MuffinLance

2/3 Meters to Swim Before Mommy Will Take You Back

Crested Otter Grebe

Gryphaquatilis Pennatauris

Known for their elaborate courtship rituals, otter grebes are also deeply caring parents. They ferry their young on their backs, teaching them to swim by diving straight out from under them. This teaches life lessons such as independence, swiftness of thought, and generational betrayal.

"I'm pretty sure that's child endangerment."
"Really?" asked Li.
"...Do we need to have the 'raising your standards' talk again, buddy?"

Artist/Creator: Bean
Writer: MuffinLance

3/8 Honey Is Not
Vegetarian

Crocodile Bumblebee

Crocodylus Bombus

Crocodile bumblebees build honeycombs near the edges of marshes. Though their primary diet consists of pollen and nectar, their larvae require significant amounts of protein to develop correctly. Specialized hunter drones work in groups to bring back flesh to the hive. The draining and clearing of wetlands for farming once pushed them towards extinction, but conservation efforts have brought back both their land and their numbers, benefitting both the crocodile bumblebees and the farmers whose crops they pollinate, and whose pests they carry off for consumption.

"You need to be careful when you separate out the honey, since some of the cells are full of meat —" said Li.
"Okay, but: honey meat."

Artist/Creator: Deathsmallcaps
Writers: Deathsmallcaps and MuffinLance

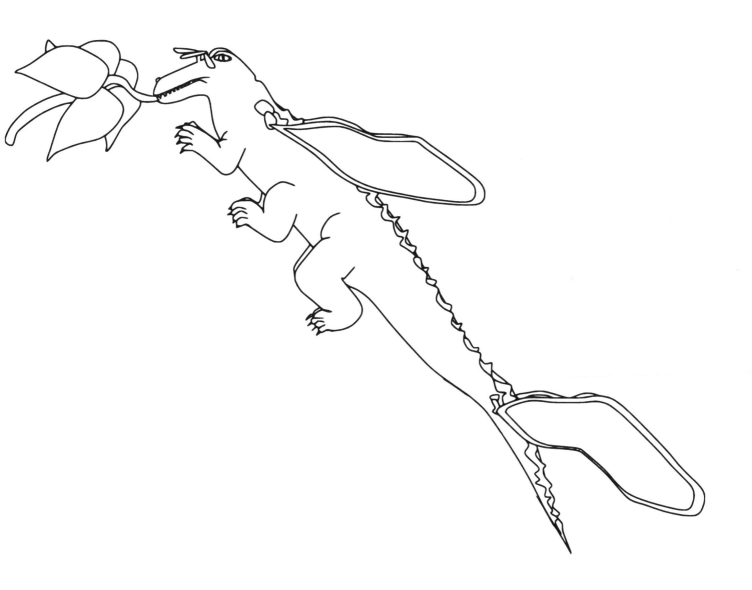

● ● ● ● ●

5/5 But Did You Close the Window That Was Above the Shed Where Anyone Could Nose Over a Box and Leap Up?

Sheep Dog

Canis Lanatus Familiaris

Sheep dogs are popular farm and family pets who will avidly herd cattle-chicken, children, and themselves. Strangers beware: they're highly territorial and will attack outsiders. They have a soft undercoat and a woolly fleece outer coat that can be sheared for wool. Though extremely intelligent and capable problem-solvers and hunters, they prefer to problem-solve ways to hunt food off peoples' plates.

"Hey, that looks like my sandwich," said his human friend. "My sandwich that was in my bag, my bag that was in my room, my room that is in the house, the house that is locked."

Artist/Creator: Kristi N.
Writers: Kristi N. and MuffinLance

**2/2 Boots Always Checked
Before Pulling On**

Honeyeater Honey Possum

Grypsaltuatimes Melipotandae

The smallest of the mammavian species, its young are born
weighing only 0.005 grams. They spend the first weeks
of their life developing in the mother's pouch and, later,
clinging to her back as she flies from flower to flower.
Candlestick banksia are a favorite. Even the adults can
easily fit in the palm of a human's hand. Largely nocturnal,
they spend their days curled up in odd nooks and crannies
for safety.

"Why aren't you wearing shoes?"
"Honey Crumble was sleeping," said Li.

Artist/Creator: CreatureThingOE
Writer: MuffinLance

Froggull

Larus Longalingua

Froggulls take great delight in squawking all day. During the spring and summer, they add sonorous croaking to the medley and regale listeners throughout the night. The general irritation and sleep deprivation thus induced makes stealing food directly from your hand both easy and satisfying.

"Why is it always my food that gets grabbed?"
"Why are you always talking instead of eating?" asked Li.

Artist/Creator: CaroloftheBell
Writer: MuffinLance

● ○ ○ ○ ○

1/5 That Feeling You
Get When the Other Guy
Gets the Girl
(and You Financed It)

Fairy Wrencoon

Procyon Passer

Fairy wrencoons are high-energy animals, constantly flit-running in search of insects to eat. During the mating season, males will pluck flower petals and steal shiny objects to present to females.

"Hey, no," said his human friend, "that is my *courtship jewelry, get back here—!"*

Artist/Creator: Celestialfeathers
Writer: MuffinLance

● ○ ○ ○ ○ ○ ○ ○ ○ ○

1/10 Put the Trash Pet
Back

Mantis Shrimp Badger

Mellivora mantis

Shrimp badgers come in many varieties and colors, their docile temperaments and undemanding scrap-food diets making them popular pets. Mantis shrimp badgers are not shrimp badgers: they're their carnivorous cousins. Mantis shrimp badgers can snap their claws straight through your yard's fence, your coop's wire, your ornamental brick wall. Mantis shrimp badgers will cut you.

"Wow. That is the prettiest shrimp badger I've ever seen. And the biggest. And those are some, uh, impressive claws. Actually maybe you should not be holding that so close to your face, where did you find that thing?"
"Madeleine was in the trash," said Li.
"Uh... huh."

Artist: Riley
Creator/Writer: MuffinLance

5/10 Cuteness Overload
and Nightmare Fuel in One
Small Package

Brush-Tailed Gecko Possum

Trichosurus Gekkopedes

The brush-tailed gecko possum is an inventive and omnivorous arboreal forager that thrives in both natural and
human spaces. They have specialized toe-pads that enable
them to adhere to even smooth vertical surfaces, and a
prehensile tail that provides balance, warmth, and security.
Their enlarged irises provide them with spectacular night
vision, aiding and abetting their nocturnal habits. Combined
with their ability to squeeze through even the smallest
opening and their fearlessness around humans, they have
become notorious for waking entire households as they
skitter noisily across the ceiling.

*"I admit, in certain circumstances, they might be adorable," said
his human friend. "But even if they were silent up there —with
the huge ears and those big black eyes just staring at me —I'm not
getting any sleep tonight, or ever again."*

Artist/Creator/Writer: Delta Shout

2/2 Teenie-Tiny Foof-Fawns
Properly Admired

Hummingdeer

Mellisugia corniger

After flaunting their aerial acrobatics to potential mates in early spring, hummingbucks grow their antlers just in time to defend their nests. As this leaves them largely flightless until their antlers shed again in late summer, the humming-does forage far and wide to bring back nectar and insects for their growing fawns.

"These deer aren't going to attack me too, are they?" asked Li. "Not effectively."

Artist/Creator: LaurJulience
Writer: MuffinLance

9/10 Family Feels

Barrier Reef Dragon

Hippocampus Octopoda

Found in small family groups, the barrier reef dragon shows a playful and cooperative nature that crosses species lines. They've even been found hunting alongside other fish, flushing out prey from tight spaces in the reef bed. Special sensors at the end of their tentacles allow them to taste anything they touch. As seen in other varieties of seahorse, the male rears the young and can be quite defensive when threatened. Direct contact with their ink is ill-advised and prompt medical attention recommended.

"Aw, hey there little guy. Oh, there are babies!"
"The red one's name is Soba," said Li. "She's the mom. This is Curry."
"They're a family. Kind of like us, huh?"

Artist/Creator/Writer: r0-ot

● ● ● ● ● ●

6/6 Wiggly Legs, Too Good
for This World

Death's Head Hawkmoth Weasel

Mustela Atropos

Also known as Little Harbingers and Thread Cutters, their skull-marked backs breed fear wherever they appear. Their nocturnal nature and habit of emitting an uncannily piercing chirp when startled have done nothing to dispel such superstitions. In reality these shy animals, like their beloved cousins the lionfish weasels, are adept hunters of pests. They tuck their wings to follow their prey into burrows, and have a sweet spot for raiding honeybee hives using their ability to mimic a bee's scent. They have six legs and brittle wings which, if injured, rarely heal. Grounded Death's Heads frequently fall prey to the superstitions of humans, as do their wingless kits.

"I'll never let them hurt you, Vermicelli," promised Li.

Artist/Creator: MariDark_Art
Writer: MuffinLance

Temple Mountains

With their proximity to both ocean and continent, the Temple Mountains maintain a pleasantly cool temperature all year round. During summer, the torrential rains that fall on its valleys and lower altitudes come down as snow in the higher reaches. Inhabitants string lines of prayer flags along pathways and in towns so the ever-present winds can carry their blessings to all.

"It's just… really nice here. Peaceful," Li said. "Too cold, though."
"You mean too hot."

● ● ● ● ○

4/5 What Has Your Pinkie
Finger Done for You Lately

Llamion

Lama Leoninus

The agile llamion is an apex predator throughout its mountain range, hunting cooperatively in small prides. Attempts to domesticate them have been met with mixed results. Knitters say their wool is worth a few fingers.

"And then he said —" started Li.
" 'It's easier to knit gloves for fewer fingers, anyway.' "

Artist/Creator: Kaitie S.
Writers: Kaitie S. and MuffinLance

6/10 Monkeys to the Face

Magpie Macaque

Macaca Pica and Macaca Gymnorhina

The magpie macaque, colloquially known as the magmonkey. Depicted are two subspecies, the northern (left) and the southern (right), Macaca Pica and Macaca Gymnorhina. They can often be found near human civilization, where they scavenge for food and leave their waste everywhere. They sometimes hunt smaller animals such as other bird hybrids, or steal eggs. A group of magmonkeys is called a gang and usually counts 10-20 animals who stroll through the streets as if they own the place. The northern magmonkey is exceptionally intelligent and very mischievous, while the southern variant is especially nasty and known to attack humans.

"How do you tell the species apart?"
"Watch which ones attack," said Li.

Artist/Creator: Jellybaby
Writers: Jellybaby and MuffinLance

4/6 Walking Composters

Vulture Goat

Capra Volturius

The vulture goat has a wide range, but is mostly found in the Temple Mountains and at the edges of the Archival Desert. Those in mountain areas tend to be more heavily feathered. They travel in small herds of a half dozen or fewer adults, which often compete for food. Vulture goats are known for eating anything and everything in their foraging, including rotting meat. Rumor has it that they headbutt other animals off cliffs and collect the carrion at the bottom. No one alive has seen this behavior.

"Let's call her Leftovers," said his human friend.

Artist/Creator: CK
Writers: CK and MuffinLance

Thylacine Moa

Dinornus Thylacinopus

Thylacine moas were the largest of the avian-marsupials. During the temple purge of the last century, refugees settled on their island in large numbers. The thylacine's previous inexperience with humans, combined with fears that they would prey on the refugees' livestock, led to them being hunted to extinction. It is said that the mocking kiwis still repeat their distinctive calls. Film buffs try to spot this sound in movies; it's a popular effect, evoking the melancholy of things lost that can never be regained. There are occasional rumors of live sightings even to the present day, though none have been substantiated.

"We're not going to find anything. Did you think we would?"
"...No," said Li.
"Look at it this way: if they were that easy to find, they really would be dead."
"...Yeah."

Artist/Creator: Deathsmallcaps
Writers: Deathsmallcaps and MuffinLance

● ● ○

2/3 Kilometers From Home

Otter Gar

Lepisosteus Lutra

Otter gars are playful and gregarious animals which can be found tussling in groups or basking in the sun by mountain lakes and streams. When hunting, they will lay still for hours before striking with blinding speed. Their pups are born with an insulating coat of fur that protects them from cold. They can grow up to three meters in length as they reach adulthood and trade fur for sterling scales. During times of drought, they've been known to flop-crawl for up to three kilometers to find a new water source.

"Knock knock."
"I don't want to hear another of your stupid—" started Li.
"Why are there fish flopping past?"
"...'Why are there fish flopping past' who?"
"That was not part of the joke, why are there giant fish flopping past and why is that one so fuzzy?*"*

Artist/Creator: Riley
Writer: MuffinLance

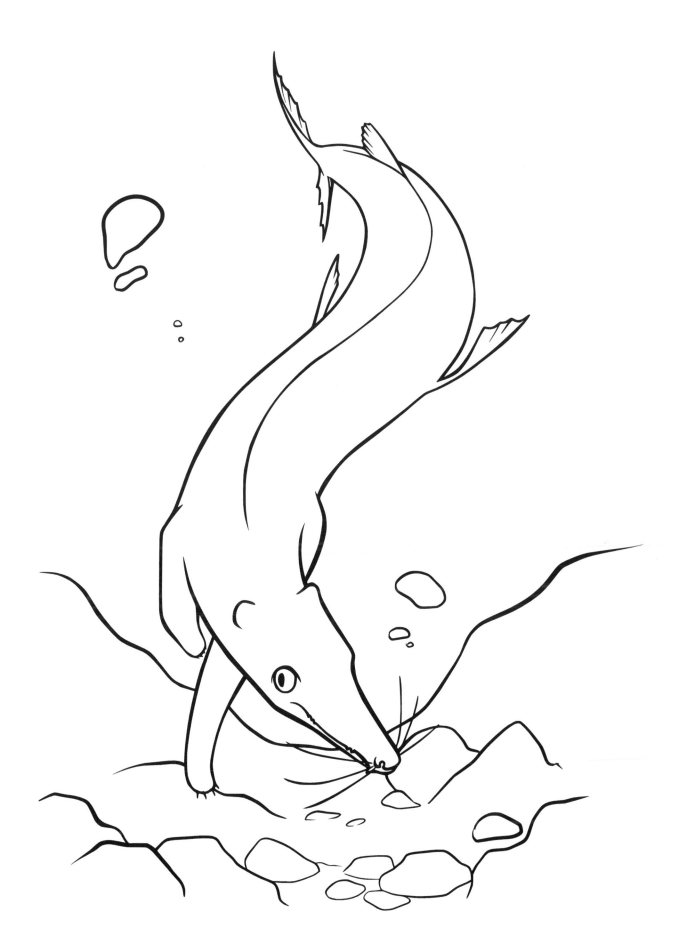

6/8 Hours of Sleep

Turtledove

Streptopelia Parmachelys

The turtledove's shell provides excellent protection from predators; many a bat cat has simply bounced off. As they age, their shells overtake more of their bodies, until they become too heavy to fly. Most wild turtledoves don't live long past this point, but domesticated doves of this distinguished age are prized for their increasingly beautiful shell patterns. Many temples encourage them to nest under verandas, as their cooing is considered akin to the sacred "om" and is a prized meditation aid.

"Sleep well?" asked Li.
"The floor started cooing at sunrise."

Artist/Creator: LaurJulience
Writer: MuffinLance

● ● ○ ○

2/4 Blood Types Sampled

Vampire Bat Hummingbird

Desmodus Trochilidinus

Vampire bat hummingbirds eat nectar almost exclusively when it's available. During the off season, they've adapted to consuming another liquid. Their sensitive ears are adept at picking up the breathing patterns of sleeping animals, after which they use the specialized heat-sensing nerves in their mouths to detect where blood runs closest to the skin. They live in colonies and exhibit social grooming and food sharing: bats who were unsuccessful at hunting on a given night are offered food by friends and family. Only males grow the distinctive tail feathers of their species. Though their length inhibits flight, they're popular with the ladies.

"I have been meaning to talk to you about that new sign in the mess hall."
"What about it?" asked Li.
" 'Be a blood donor?' "

Artist/Creator: Foofymonkey
Writer: MuffinLance

9/10 Thorns in Use,
Room for One More

Shrike Degu

Degugryps Transfodiens

The Little Songbutcher. Shrike degus form communal colonies, communicating with each other using more than fifteen distinct calls. By working together, they're able to nurse and protect the colony's pups, defend their territory, and build towering larders stocked with hundreds of impaled victims. They prefer to nest in thorn trees surrounded by open ground, so that their sentinels have a line of sight for hunting and defense, and so their competitors can look upon their works and despair.

"Chittering murder tree."
"The chitter is their call for 'friend'," Li informed him.
"Chittering murder tree."

Artist/Creator: MariDark_Art
Writers: MariDark_Art and MuffinLance

4/5 Eat Your Nightmares

Moth Dove

Columba Morpheus

Though moth doves come in astoundingly beautiful colors and patterns, their habit of invading wardrobes and libraries to lay their eggs—and their chickerpillars' healthy appetites—have made them a reviled pest from town to temple. Their large cocoons, if fried, make a gooey delicacy. Though the adults fly mostly during the day, they are found roosting in homes primarily through the soft sounds they make in the night, leading to their association with both insomnia and dreams.

"So basically, kids here have monsters in their closets," said his human friend. "They're real. And they're edible?"

Artist/Creator: J.B. MothDove
Writers: Titanic-Ente and MuffinLance

●

1/1 Somebody Here Has
Some History with the Moon

Marsupial Spinebill Mouse

Murirhynchus Halucinatii

A local legend claims that in the Before, the spinebill mouse
carried the moon in her pouch until it was ready to be born.
The new moon is simply a child returning to earth to visit
its mother. Actual spinebill mice forage most heavily at dusk
and are important pollinators of many night-blooming
plants. Their pups are moon-gray for the first few months
of their lives. If a person harms a spinebill mouse, they
must apologize to the moon for the harm done to its family.

"How do you apologize to the moon?"
"Why do you need to know?" asked Li.

Artist/Creator: CreatureThingOE
Writers: CreatureThingOE and MuffinLance

● ○ ○ ○ ○
1/5 Poor Hair Stylist,
Would Not Recommend

Iguana Owl

Alariguana Mentupanniculi

Iguana owls can be found foraging for plants or basking on rocks outside their cliffside nests during the day. At night, they take to the air to hunt. As they are too heavy to achieve lift from the ground, they will first climb a cliff face or tree to wait, then swoop down to the kill.

"Why did it attack my hair*?"*
"Why did it think your hair was a small animal?" asked Li.

Artist/Creator: Vanessa Landolt
Writer: MuffinLance

● ○ ○ ○ ○ ○

1/6 The Babies Do the
Throwing-Themselves
Thing Too

Hedgehog Woodpecker

Dryocopus Ericius

The hedgehog woodpecker's distinctive quills are more
numerous in unfledged chicks, who curl into spiny balls when
threatened. As their flight feathers grow in, the majority
of their quills grow out, until they're left with only an adult's
back quills. During the winter, when insects are scarce,
they hibernate in tree hollows and old animal burrows. When
threatened, hedgehog woodpeckers may briefly hurl
themselves backwards to startle predators and strike with
their quills before flying away.

*"Do you want to tell me how you got all the teeny-tiny needle
stabs in your hand, or do you want me to tell you not to mess with
nests?" asked his human friend.*

Artist/Creator: LaurJulience
Writer: MuffinLance

10/10 Their Auras Are
as Colorful as Their Wings

Emperor Tortoise Moth

Saturnichelys Coccinella

Young tortoise moths hatch soft-shelled and light, allowing them to fly on their colorful wings for the first few years of their lives. As they grow from 5 cm to their adult length of 83 cm, their shell hardens and thickens, rendering them flightless. Adults' wings are kept partially tucked inside their shell, brought out primarily for courtship displays. Wing types and patterns vary even within the same species. Combined with its docile nature and the soft, moth-like fluff on its head, its showy wings have made it popular in the pet trade.

"Okay, but the little ones are soft-shelled, right? But the shell is their spine, right? So what, they're the freaky acrobats of the turtle world?"
"You've seen caterpillars squirm before," said Li. "Like that, but a tortoise."

Artist/Creator: ThimbleHouses
Writers: ThimbleHouses and MuffinLance

3/3 Toe-Palates in Need
of Cleansing

Butterfly Raven

Catagusa Sepulcralis

Butterfly ravens feature prominently in local tales of death
and rebirth. Eggs are laid in wildflower patches during the
spring, with the meat of scavenged carcasses tucked lovingly
around host plants. Their chickerpillars need both food
sources to successfully pupate. Adult butterfly ravens remain
on watch in the area throughout their growth, ready to
welcome their newest flock members into the sky. As human
settlements grow, their inhabitants carefully maintain the
sanctity of the butterfly ravens' preferred meadows, which
are used for sky burials. To die in the spring while the
chickerpillars are still feeding is considered a sign that one
will be favored in their next life. Local farmers have significantly more mixed feelings on these animals: adults have
taste receptors on their feet and often help themselves to
the best of the harvest.

"Bleck."
"Did that bird taste my shoulder?" asked Li. *"Did that bird taste
my shoulder and* bleck?*"*

Artist/Creator: PoCATo
Writers: PoCATo and MuffinLance

**3/5 Let Their Cleanliness
Be an Example to Us All**

Coonlion Fish

Procyon Aculeus

Also known as the Spiny Trash Panda, coonlion fish are intelligent problem solvers. They will intelligently find wherever you're hiding your food and problem solve their way inside. They take all liberated foodstuffs to the nearest stream, both to give it a thorough washing and to allow themselves a quick escape route should the original owner take offense. Between their adept swimming and their venomous spines, most are too wise to bother.

"I understand I lost to a raccoon. But does it have to sit there, washing my poor lunch in front of me?"
"It needs to get off your human germs," said Li.
"...That's fair."

Artist/Creator: CaroloftheBell
Writer: MuffinLance

● ● ● ○ ○

3/5 Who Wouldn't Be
Jealous of that
Slither-Swagger

Anteater Snake

Vermilingua Calliophis

These slithery animals, despite the potent venom in their bite, are a welcome sight in any town. Though they have never been formally domesticated, they show little fear of humans and have few reasons to: their habit of traveling from garden to garden devouring all pests in their wake has endeared them to locals since time immemorial. Historical evidence suggests they used to migrate to lower, warmer altitudes during the winter, but current populations prefer to take up residence in the rafters of barns. Local folklore tells that they whisper inspiration into the household they choose. Being chosen by an anteater snake for the winter is considered a blessing and, regardless of whether anyone in the family goes on to create great works of music or art, their livestock will spend a winter free from flea mice. Locals always maintain a respectful distance from their venomous muses.

"Why is everything super deadly also super pretty?"
"...Are you jealous?" asked Li.

Artist: Bean; Creator: Kibeth3
Writer: MuffinLance

○ ○

0/2 Wouldn't It Be a Shame
to Skip Leg Day

Killer Pteroroo

Dsungaripterus Marsupilia

This marsupial's powerful hind legs launch it into the air, where it promptly fall-glides back to the ground. They nest in mobs on lower plains and valleys. Mobs work in concert to herd prey, standing on their hind legs and flashing their wings to startle animals and physically block their escape routes. Though they typically use this tactic to flush out small prey, their herding has occasionally caused larger animals to stampede, sometimes straight over cliffs. It's from these mass kills that they've earned their name.

"Okay, but can we talk about those muscles? Leg day is every day," said his human friend.

Artist/Creator: CreatureThingOE
Writers: CreatureThingOE and MuffinLance

10/10 Ceiling Cats Judging
Your Petting Technique

Bat Cat

Felivespertilio Tenebrarum

These affectionate animals live in large colonies, making
them the animal hoarder's dream. They nest densely in the
rafters of homes they've adopted, forming a fuzzy mass
of sleepy bodies during the day and a hibernating layer of
roof insulation come winter. Once trained to use the home-
owner's garden as a litter box, they provide both an endless
source of guano as fertilizer and a scratching deterrent to
weeds. Bat cat aficionados can be identified by their habit
of walking through houses with both arms raised, ready
to pet any pretty kitties who might be dangling there. This
behavior is greeted with indulgent laughter in local homes
and concerned puzzlement outside the bat cat's native
range.

"Please stop petting the ceiling."
"But it's purring," said Li.

Artist/Creator: Vanessa Landolt
Writer: MuffinLance

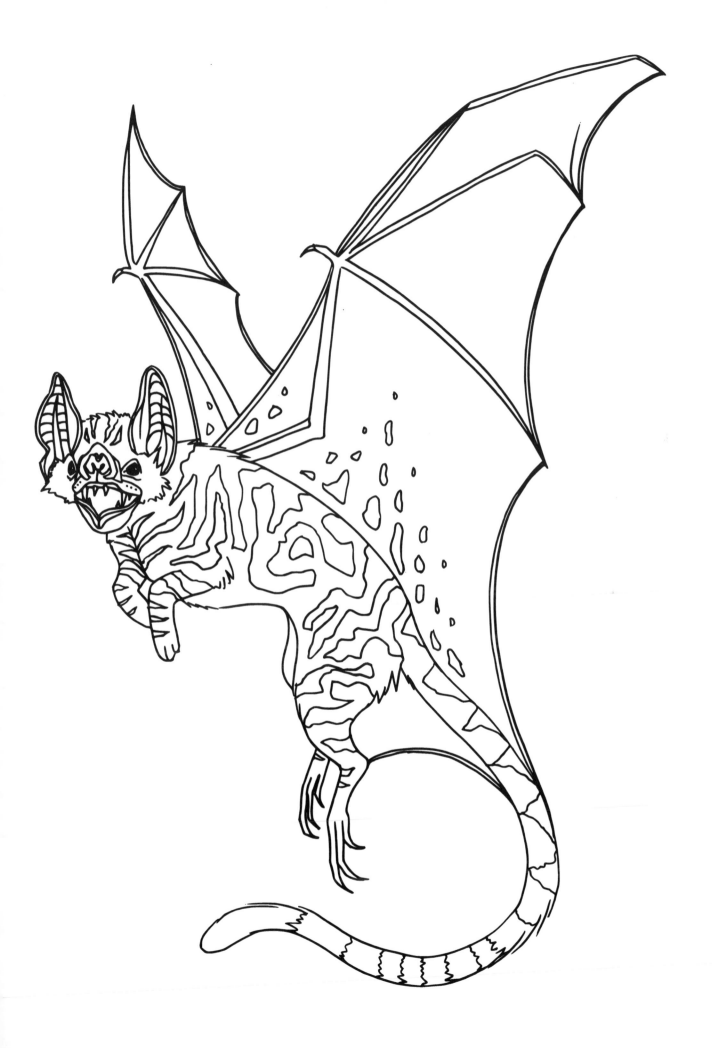

Wayward Swamp

Large bugs. Large predators. Little room for mistakes. Some have attempted to drain the swamp for farmland. Some have even been seen again.

"This place is terrible.".
"It is literally the worst."
It did not matter which of them said what, as both statements
were mutually agreed upon as completely true and unbiased
assessments of the ~~Worst~~ Wayward Swamp.

● ○

1/2 People Here Can Go
Get Eaten

Frobbit

Piscinalagus Cuniculus

Two frobbits are a pair. A group of frobbits is a fluffle.
Fluffles, left to procreate, are an army. With no set breeding
season and the ability to lay up to 50,000 eggs at a time,
frobbits should march a furry line across the world. They
don't. They haven't run out of food in their native range
yet, either. This implies a number of predators within the
Wayward Swamp whose hunger can regularly swallow
an army. This implication is correct.

"...Just get it over with," said Li.
"Ahem. So... you're saying all those frobbits croaked?"

Artist/Creator: stardumb
Writer: MuffinLance

● ○ ○ ○ ○
1/5 Is That Really the
Important Question Here

Hippo Scorpion

Pandinus Hippopotamodus

This semi-aquatic giant is known for its aggression and startling agility. It can strike with its stinger in the blink of an eye while hiding below the waterline.

"But who would win," asked his human friend, "a hippo scorpion or a murder moose?"

Artist/Creator: KitKatalaya
Writers: KitKatalaya and MuffinLance

**2/3 Less Rude Than
Killing You**

Hummingbird Octopus

Anthracothorax Octopodiformodus

It is generally accepted that the most dangerous predators of the Wayward Swamp are those that dwell in the water. This is not to say that travelers are safe on land. When the hummingbird octopus detects vibrations through its sensitive tentacles, it launches into the air on its fleshy wings and delivers a myriad of venomous stings to whatever walks above. As they rarely have time to finish eating their prey before larger competition arrives, hummingbird octopi have adapted from their ancestors' nectar-sipping to supping on redder wines. Some victims even survive their stings, if they can recover before the scavengers arrive.

"Did I just get dine and dashed by a birdopus?" asked his human friend. "Rude."

Artist/Creator: Dragon Harris
Writers: Dragon Harris and MuffinLance

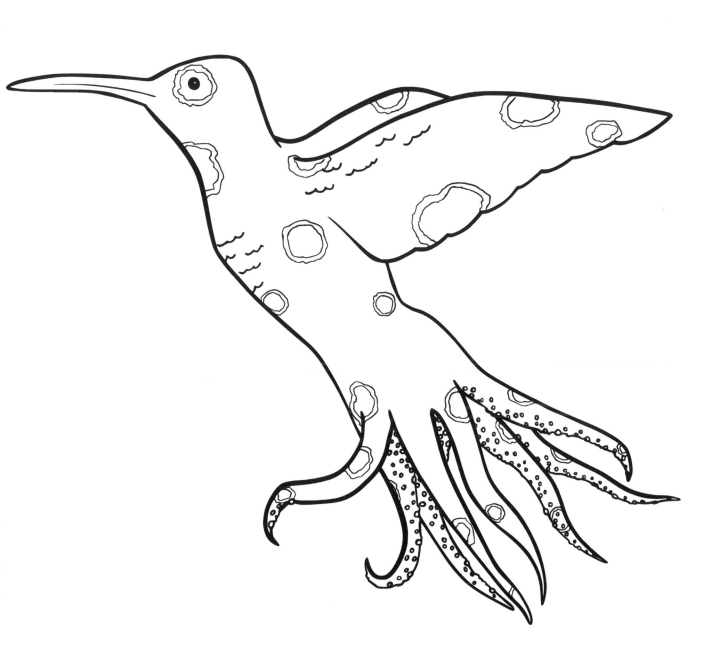

● ● ○ ○ ○

2/5 Human Friend
Definitely Could Have
Drawn Them Better

Monarch Fox

Danaus Vulpes

Among the gentlest of swamp dwellers, what the monarch fox lacks in ferocity it makes up for in indigestion: from birth onwards, it regularly supplements its diet with milk-weed-nightshade, to whose poisons it is immune. Its predators are not. Few species dare do more than admire these graceful beauties as they daintily dine on nectar and small insects. Their annual migration corresponds with that of the continental monarch elephant. The two have been observed flocking together as they voyage into the unexplored depths of the swamp's heart.

"When you showed me that sketch, I expected a slightly different scale."
"What? I drew them to scale," said Li.
"And yet, you failed to mention that the flowers were me-sized."

Artist: Moira H.; Creator: Kibeth3
Writer: MuffinLance

○ ○ ○ ○ ○
0/5 Sweet Dreams Are
Made of Chitter-Screams

Fox Centipede

Lithobius Vulpinius

These forest dwellers can grow up to a meter long and use
their acute sense of smell to find their prey. At night
they vocalize with surprisingly loud chittering screams.

"Why does the night sound like it wants to kill me?"
"If anything wanted to kill you, it would be quieter," said Li.

Artist/Creator: KitKatalaya
Writers: KitKatalaya and MuffinLance

● ● ● ● ○

4/5 Piglet-Tadpoles in a
Tree Above You,
Better Watch Out for Mama

Froghog

Ranaper Maculagula

Froghogs use their sticky tongues to pluck leaves and fruits that would otherwise be out of reach. They seek shelter in hidden burrows, either ones they've dug or those abandoned by other animals, and rest with their tusked heads towards the entrance. Those who stumble upon them can expect a vicious charge.

"You forgot to mention the sticky-footed climbing thing."
"The what?" asked Li.
"Look up."

Artist/Creator: Misti_Future
Writers: Misti_Future and MuffinLance

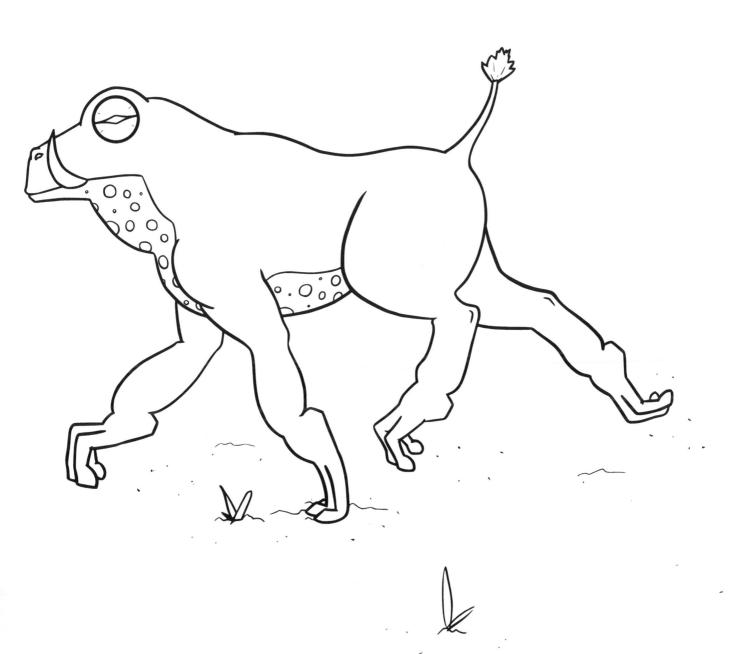

● ○ ○ ○ ○

1/5 They Would Like You
Better if You Didn't Try to
Stop Them

Great Crested Newt Beaver

Castor Triturus

Great crested newtbeavers are the bane of farmers and fo-
resters who make their livelihoods at the Wayward Swamp's
edges. A female newtbeavers will lay up to a hundred eggs
each spring, which she and the father will cooperatively care
for until the tadpoles complete their metamorphosis.
Expectant parents will construct massive dams and lodges
to accommodate their entire family. While the majority
of newtbeavers fall to predators within the first two years
of life, those that survive will leave home to seek out
partners and new places to live, pushing the edges of the
swamp outward one busy beaver at a time.

*"I would like these things better if they weren't helping the
terrifying swamp take over the world," said his human friend.*

Artist/Creator: Jellybaby
Writers: Jellybaby and MuffinLance

○ ○ ○ ○ ○

0/5 Don't Go Towards
the Light

Goldjaw

Malacosteus Lemiscatus

Goldjaws live in the brackish water between swamp and sea, where they exhibit a symbiotic relationship with thorny ethereal slugs. The slugs attract other fish with their bioluminescence and tempting squirms, at which point the goldjaws paralyze and consume them. The slugs feed upon the scraps. Both goldjaws and slugs can grow to ridiculous lengths, should they survive the hazards of their own bait-and-switch hunting strategy.

"There was just a cat fish swimming in that water," said Li.
"Yep."
"And now there's not."
"Nope."

Artist/Creator: SnazzyAddie
Writer: SnazzyAddie and MuffinLance

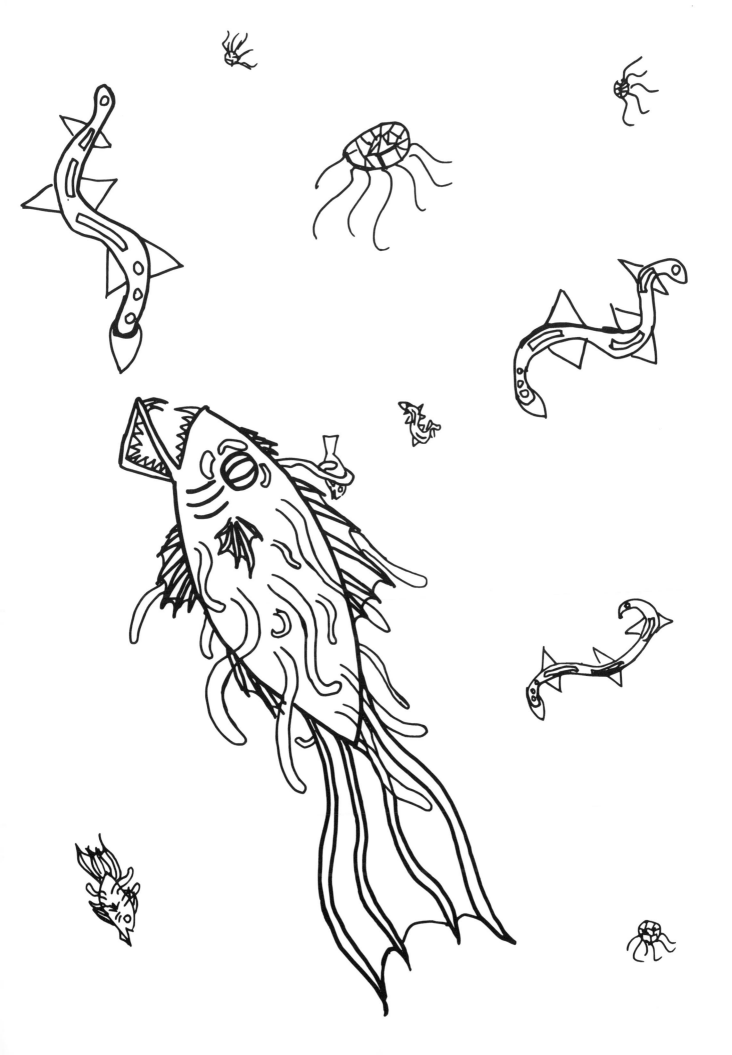

2/2 Ears Swiveled
Your Way, Go Ahead, Keep
Talking

Bush Viper Bat

Pteropus Squamiger

Bush viper bats have wingspans in excess of a meter and can fly up to 40 kilometers per hour. They will eat nectar, pollen, and fruit, but are primarily ambush predators. Nocturnal hunters, they hang upside down by their prehensile tails and strike at their prey with alarming speed. Rodents, birds, frogs, and reptiles are preferred. Though small, their venom is extremely potent.

"Can we please talk about this swamp's definition of 'small'?"
said his human friend.

Artist/Creator: Nicole H.
Writers: Nicole H. and MuffinLance

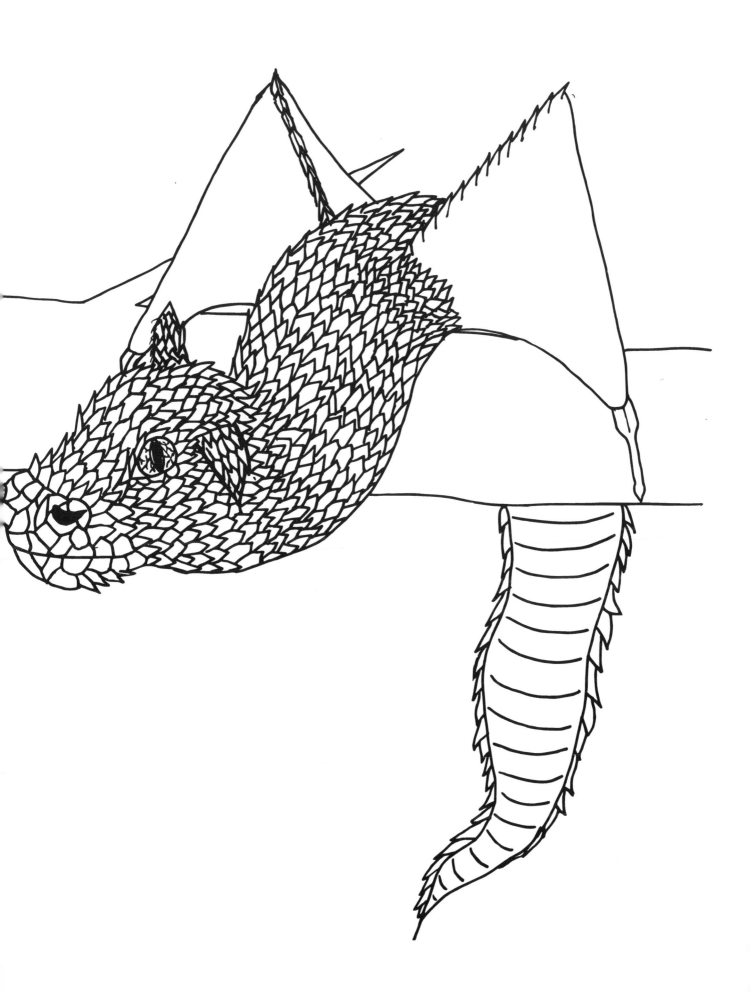

Cat Fish

Felix Weticus

Mimicking the cries of young animals, it lures prey to the water where they can be dragged under and drowned. Cat fish can grow up to a meter in length from nose to tail. They generally hunt other fish and small mammals, though they've been known to catch prey up to four times their size. Like all cats, they enjoy fitting themselves into improbable spaces.

"Would you get out of my sleeping bag? It's not my fault you sacrificed yours to the Fluffy Things You Shouldn't Pet."
"...That's not me," said Li.

Artist/Creator/Writer: r0-ot

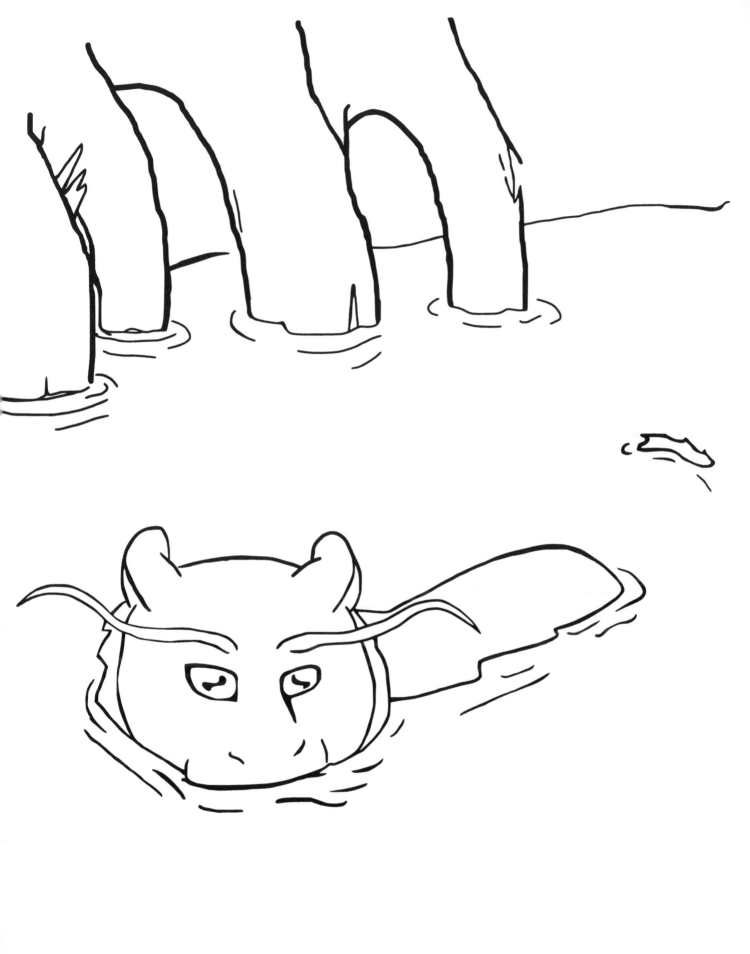

7/7 Words Added to Their Repertoire

Parrot Hyena

Psittacrocuta Maculosus

Parrot hyenas have the uncanny ability to mimic human speech and are intelligent enough to use their ill-gotten words in context. Though they supplement their diets with berries and nuts, they show a certain delight in hunting more mobile prey. Flocks roost high in trees, cackling and chatting until a target is spotted; then they'll swiftly swoop-pounce to the kill, devouring even the bones of their prey.

"Hey, what's that, hey."
"...Was that you?" asked Li.
"Look up, pretty birds, pretty, look."
"...That was not me," said his human friend.
"Run-they're-coming, run-they're-coming, run-they're—"

Artist/Creator: Stydealized
Writers: Stydealized and MuffinLance

Moth Bat

Charontotis Ominata

Though their eyes can only distinguish light and dark, their sense of smell and their echolocation make them expert navigators. Their sonar pulses are intense enough to stun their prey mid-air. Folklore holds that, should a traveler find a moth bat crossing their path, they can number their remaining days by how many more they see before their journey's end. It's a local custom to hold a bonfire the night before a journey, in the hopes that uncountable moth bats will be attracted by the flames.

"So fires here mean 'we hope you don't *die',"* said his human friend. *"Good to know."*

Artist/Creator: PoCATo
Writers: PoCATo, Titanic-Ente, and MuffinLance

5/5 The Dream of Every
Tourist-Town Native

Croc-of-the-Rock

Crocodylus Plumifrontalia

While croc-of-the-rocks are usually elusive animals, they gather each winter in the coastal marshes for lek displays, wherein numerous males compete for their females' attentions. With the flashy colors of their head crests and their elaborate rolling dances, tourists are prone to forgetting that these absurdly behaving animals are actually predators. Locals call this annual culling of their visitors the Tourist Tithe.

"So they feed tourists to crocodiles, is what you're saying."
"No," said Li, "they just rent out boats and collect them again when they're empty."
"So they make tourists pay for the experience, is what you're saying."

Artist/Creator: Cally P.
Writers: Cally P. and MuffinLance

-/- The Negative Space
Carved by a Nightmare
Unseen

Drop Worm

Phascolarctos Grassator

Also known as the Highwayman Koala. It's said that their mandibles, once locked into flesh, retract fully down their throat while dragging their still-struggling prey. It's said they grow additional arm and leg segments with each year of their long, long lives. It's said they give great hugs; you'll never want for another. This is all hypothetical, of course, since it's said that they're only legend. Some go so far as to claim that the locals have invented them entirely; that drop worms are just a joke played upon gullible tourists. It's said that the great sequoia-eucalyptus groves never ring with the screams of drop worm disbelievers. There's no trace anyone ventured there at all, really.

"But they are *just a joke, right?" asked his human friend. "If no one's ever seen them and lived, how does anyone know they're there?"*

Artist/Creator: CreatureThingOE
Writers: CreatureThingOE and MuffinLance

10/10 Minutes Spent
Staring Prior to Comment

Butterbeaver

Castor Decorescaudae

Considered the less destructive cousin of the newtbeaver, butterbeavers leave the water only to lay their eggs on nearby vegetation. The rest of their short lives are spent swimming among the swamp's numerous aquatic plants, flitting only briefly above the water to drink nectar from flowers or sun themselves on lotus-lily pads. They live for only a few weeks, with several generations passing within the space of a year. Their tails come in a dizzying array of colors and patterns that are said to hypnotize the viewer.

"They're pretty, I'll grant, but hypnotism isn't real."
"Look away, then say that again," said Li.
"Naw, I'm good."

Artist/Creator: CK
Writers: CK and MuffinLance

9/10 Physicians
Recommend

Anteater Wasp

Vespa Vermilingua

This fluffy wasp's tongue is too large to fit into its body along-side a full meal. It's possible to estimate how much and how recently one has eaten by how much of its tongue is held outside. Though it lacks a stinger, its sticky tongue is covered in a mild paralytic. As this also induces temporary numb-ness to the affected area, local healers keep colonies and will brush sugar water onto the limbs of patients prior to minor medical operations in order to solicit their services.

"Haven't they heard of anesthetics?" asked Li.
"What do you think anesthetics are made from?"

Artist/Creator: CK
Writers: CK and MuffinLance

● ○ ○ ○ ○

1/5 Flamingos With
Black-Tipped Feathers,
It Was Just a Little Taste

Snapping Flamingo

Phoenicoparrus Commordetus

These ornery creatures have come under threat from poachers in recent years, as their showy feathers are in high demand. Alive, they're used as breeding stock for pet shows, being cross-bred with the more docile painted stork to achieve mild-tempered animals whose shells are a match for their feathers. Dead, their feathers are used as ornamentation, particularly on hats. Unique colors can be induced by strictly controlling their diet, though this is rarely healthy for the birds long-term.

"So let me guess, the red ones eat blood?" said his human friend.
"No, digested blood is black."
"...Why do you know that?"

Artist/Creator: E. L. Perkins
Writers: E. L. Perkins and MuffinLance

●
1/1 Pairs of Pants in Need
of Mending

Tiger Fish

Hydrocynus Tigris

Unlike true fish, the tiger fish is warm-blooded and has a thin coat of slick fur that allows it to slip through the roots of various trees easily. Their prey includes their slightly smaller cousin, the cat fish. In times of scarcity, their lungs allow them to leave the water and hunt for food on land for short periods of time. Croc-of-the-rocks, froghogs, and humans enter their menus at such times. They must return to the water before their gills dehydrate or risk a slow death out of water, as their cartilaginous skeletons are ill suited to permanent life on land.

"There's a good girl," said Li. "You just needed a little water, didn't you?"
"Are you watering the thing that tried to eat me?"
"I'm watering Mochi."
"You named *the thing that tried to eat me?"*

Artist/Writer: r0-ot; Creator: Kibeth3

**7/8 Unblinking Eyes
of Momma Bird Watching**

Spider Toucan

Ramphatos Octi-oculus

When fruit begins to grow on their favorite trees, a small flock of spider toucans will work cooperatively to encase an entire grove in a loose web. This protects their future dinner and catches a few snacks in the meantime. Their nests are built and their young reared in the safety of that year's web.

"Here I am. Stuck to a tree. You could help."
"You're too big to eat," said Li.
"Not too big for them to try."
"They're babies.*"*

Artist/Creator: LaurJulience
Writer: MuffinLance

Archival Desert

Rolling dunes and secret oases form an arid landscape vibrant with hidden life. Its people understand that knowledge means survival; they carefully preserve their own teachings and place a high trade value on new information. Scholars travel far to read the most ancient of tomes from all lands, perfectly preserved by the dry desert air. The bodies of those that die in the desert's depths are preserved for the ages and may lay mummified for centuries before they're found, if they ever are.

"Nature's jerky," said his human friend.
"You're not allowed to talk anymore," said Li.

○ ○

0/2 Jawbones,
Who Needs 'Em

Snake Urchin

Maxillabeccus Ericius

Snake urchins bury themselves in the sand to wait for prey. Their beak-jaw, strong enough to crush even rocks, makes swift work of bone. When threatened, they curl into a protective ball of spikes. The sound produced by this action has led to their other common name, the Rattle Hedgehog.

"At least they don't do the freaky swallow-you-whole thing that swamp snakes do," said his human friend. "They'll just grind you into a meaty paste."

Artist/Creator: KitKatalaya
Writers: KitKatalaya and MuffinLance

**8/8 Legs Busy
Investigating Your Hair,
Free Scalp Massage**

Tarantula Bat

Pteropelma Lapsodos

Tarantula bats seek out local high points such as the tops of bushes and trees. Their wings allow them to glide through the air, herding insects into their webs. People who stand still too long may be mistaken for cacti and can expect a visit from young tarantula bats seeking an unclaimed nesting spot.

"This is the least horrifying thing that has happened to me in recent memory," said his human friend. "That is its own kind of horror."

Artist/Creator: KitKatalaya
Writers: KitKatalaya and MuffinLance

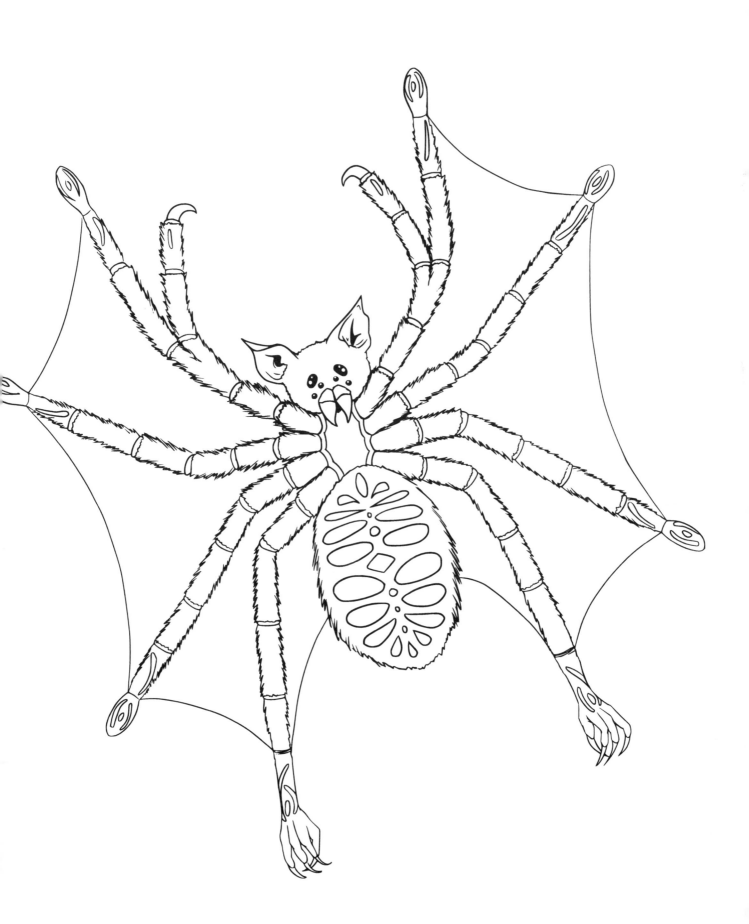

**4/4 Big Siblings Ready
to Intervene**

Owl Wolf

Parragryphus Lupinus

Groups of owl wolves, called parliaments, are composed of
parents and their children. The past season's puppylets
will remain with their family for two or more years, helping
to raise their younger siblings and gain hunting experience
before leaving to form parliaments of their own. Most species
sleep the scorching days away in their burrows, coming
out at night for the hunt.

*"I'm normally against bringing dangerous animals back with
us," said his human friend. "But those puppylets are really fluffy,
and is it really kidnapping if you're adopting?"*

Artist/Creator: AlyssumGrey
Writers: AlyssumGrey and MuffinLance

Kangaroo Bird

Macropus Rostratus

Though kangaroo birds as a whole come in an astonishing
variety of sizes, colors, and diets, the desert kangaroo bird
is most commonly the kangaroo kestrel. They live in large
groups and hunt small rodents and lizards. Kangaroo
kestrels are drawn to wildfires, where they can easily pick
off prey as it flees the flames.

"Attracted to wildfires, huh."
"It was one time," said Li.

Artist/Creator: Chaotic-Energy; Art Clean Up: Neko265
Writer: MuffinLance

∞/∞ nope nope
nope nope—

Jewel Shrike Wasp

Ampulex Lanius

The strikingly colored jewel shrike wasp is a solitary hunter that builds its roosts in thorn bushes. Like their cousins the shrike degu, they maintain an impaled larder for later eating. The jewel shrike, however, prefers to outsource its childcare. The female will hunt a rabbit-roach, delivering two potent stings: the first to paralyze and the second—expertly delivered to targeted sections of its brain—rendering it unable to even contemplate fleeing. The jewel shrike will then lead her new foster mother back to a pre-prepared burrow, where she will wall the roach inside after laying an egg on its body. Her child will emerge from the burrow some weeks later, leaving the husked surrogate behind.

"...Nope," said his human friend.

Artist/Creator: Cara
Writer: MuffinLance

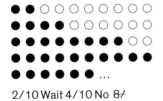

2/10 Wait 4/10 No 8/
I meant 16

Hopping Mouse Wren

Troglodytes Assultimus

The hopping mouse wren is a small prey animal with many unique features to help it evade predators and survive the arid environment where it lives. The ultimate tactic it uses is to reproduce as quickly as possible, particularly when there is an overabundance of food sources. This is known as a 'population explosion'.

"There were only two yesterday," said Li. "How many are there now?"
"You really don't want to know..."

Artist/Creator/Writer: Delta Shout

2/4 Sentries
Listening for You

Harekat

Herpestidae Lepus

Harekats build massive tunnel systems under the arid grasslands of the desert's edge. They form clans of up to forty members who share in duties of kit-rearing and lookouts, and communicate through a rich variety of noises. With their acute ears, they can hear prey moving from up to three miles away. As one of the smallest predators in the desert, they rely on their swift hop-lopping gait to reach their target, dispatch it, and return to safety before anything larger can find them.

"What are those specks, some kind of bunny?" asked his human friend. "Yeah, definitely bunnies. Fast bunnies. Very fast bunnies."

Artist/Creator: ThisCat
Writers: ThisCat and MuffinLance

9/10 Only a Cat of a
Different Coat

Jumping Spidercat

Phidippus Felis

Jumping spidercats, those ubiquitously popular pets (and invasive predators), hail originally from the Archival Desert. It's theorized that they self-domesticated around eight thousand years ago, when the natives of the region first developed agriculture. The grains they grew attracted pests, who attracted spidercats, and a mutually beneficial arrangement was born. The common spidercat fits in a human's palm. The incredible variety of coat colorings is a relatively modern development and is, genetically speaking, one of the few differences between domestic and wild spidercats, who can still be found pouncing prey in their ancestral home.

"I'm ninety percent sure that is not *someone's pet kitty."*
"I'm ninety percent sure there isn't a difference," said Li.

Artist/Creator: Jellybaby
Writers: Jellybaby and MuffinLance

○
0/1 Murders Here,
Just Keep Walking

Gila Raven

Heloderma Alatato

Though folklore tells of winged monsters descending on caravans, gila ravens are actually quite sedate creatures, who can be found curling up in sheltered spaces with the rest of their conspiracy during the hottest hours of the day. Adults can reach an excess of a half-meter in length, with a wing-span twice that. These flightless reptavians use their wings to regulate temperature for their featherless fledglings, providing shade during the day and a comforting cover at night. They pose little threat to travelers who keep their distance. Unfortunately, their native curiosity can lead them close to human camps and settlements. Their venomous bite is said to be one of the most painful in the world, but is rarely lethal.

"Okay, but can we talk about these group names? 'Conspiracy',
'unkindness', 'murder' —"
"Murders aren't gila ravens," Li said. "You're thinking of recluse
crows. Look, there's one behind you."
"Please never say 'there's a murder behind you' ever again."
"I didn't, there's only one. Oh, wait."
"…"
"It's okay, conspiracies eat murders."

Artist/Creator: Dragon Harris
Writer: MuffinLance

○ ○ ○ ○ ○
0/5 Poachers Heard
From Again

Oyster Snake

Epicrates Ostreicaput

This shy filter feeder lives in the water of desert oases. They burrow their long bodies deep into the wet sands, leaving only their heads exposed. A shadow or a poke will send them rapidly retreating into their tunnels. Local lore has long held that to kill one is to wish a curse upon the water it lived in. Recent scientific studies have backed the superstition: in addition to filtering nitrogen and other wastes, they also filter the larvae of heartworm-mosquitoes, greatly reducing outbreaks of coronary malaria.

"But aren't their pearls really popular?"
"If you want to start a fight, try wearing one here," said Li.

Artist/Creator: lyditist
Writer: MuffinLance

2/2 Kneecaps in Their Back, Warn a Frog First

Scorpion Frog

Ranascorpius Ranunculus

Oasis visitors beware: scorpion frogs breed in abundance in even the smallest puddle of water, with adults burrowing into the damp sand for their afternoon siesta. Many a traveler has made the mistake of kneeling on buried scorpion frogs when they go to drink. Locals view them with respectful fondness, as they inhabit the same locations as oyster snakes and do a much better job of defending them. Scorpion frogs take on the role of guardians and judges of character in folklore. They are said to love dance and song, which they partake in with great enthusiasm each night when the sun goes down. The wise traveler will approach any oasis with an offering of both if they wish to gain the blessing of the Singing Sentries. In reality, the noise and vibrations give any buried scorpion frogs enough warning to hop away.

"I am not dancing my way to the water," said Li.
"See I wasn't going to either, but if it would embarrass you..."

Artist/Creator: LaurJulience
Writer: MuffinLance

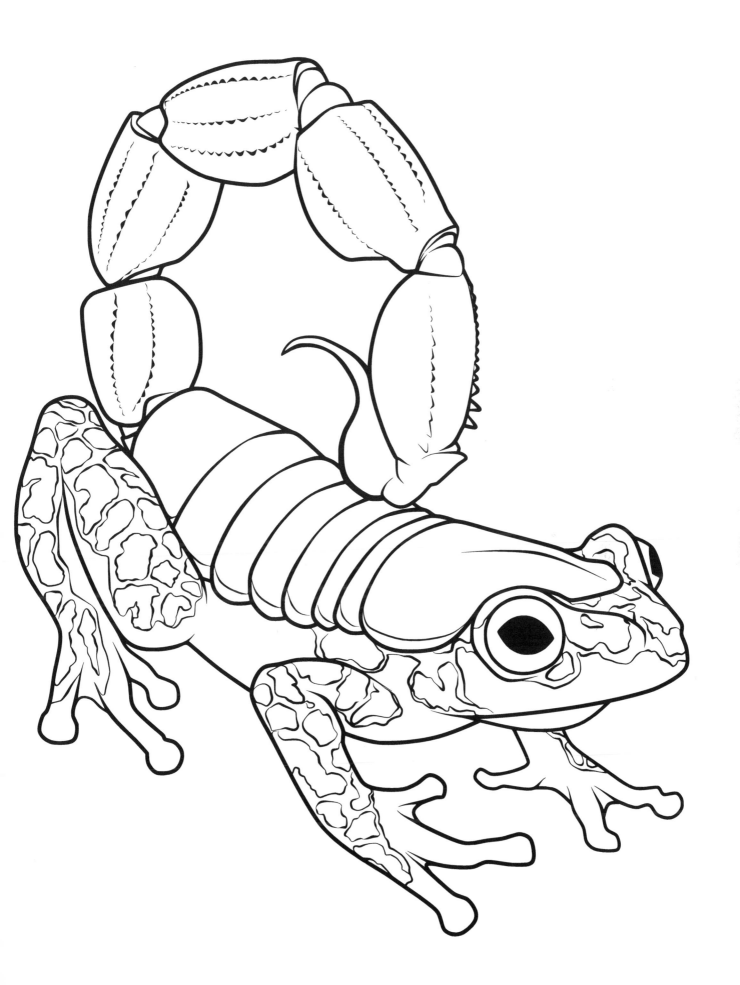

● ● ● ● ●

5/5 It Was the Best of Hats,
It Was the Worst of Hats

Serpentfly

Dipsadiplax Subridens

Serpentflies skim low over the ground, dragging their long tails after them as bait to lure out scorpion frogs and other small animals. Serpentflies enjoy sunning themselves in local high spots including cacti, rock outcroppings, and the tops of travelers' heads. They rarely strike humans unless one foolishly tries to move them. Some serpentflies make a habit of following humans to hunt the smaller animals they spook out. If such hunts are successful, they may return to the same person again and again.

"It's happy to see you," said Li.
"I'm not happy to see it."

Artist/Creator: ThisCat
Writer: ThisCat and MuffinLance

3/5 Nobles Chased Off (2/5 Confused Nobles Adopted into the Flock)

Peacock Goat

Pavo Ungulatus

These showy animals live on the Archival Desert's rocky plateaus. There was a recent trend among wealthy continentals to import these flying ungulates to roam their pristine gardens. The trend ended when they realized an urban peacock goat's diet could easily expand from their natural scrub brush to include ornamental plants, clothes, and various building materials. In their native range, peacock bucks are belligerently territorial, particularly against their cousins the lion peacocks. They apply the same ferocity to anything that dares match them in color and splendor.

"And that was the end of His Majesty's garden parties," said his human friend.

Artist/Creator: sheepscot
Writers: sheepscot and MuffinLance

● ● ● ● ● ● ● ● ● ● ● ●

12/12 Fuzzy Faces
in Your Food

Scorpion Rat

Rodoscorpius Rattus

These intelligent animals make inquisitive pets, though their popularity is dampened by their historical association with disease and famine. Scorpion rats give birth to live pups, who ride on their mother's back for days until their exoskeletons harden. They form colonies of up to a hundred animals spread across a dozen closely placed tunnel-nests. In folklore, they occupy a place opposite the scorpion frog: instead of righteous defenders, they're depicted as thieving scoundrels, constantly seeking to steal all a community has gathered. Wild scorpion rats are exterminated whenever they're found nesting near humans.

"So I just opened our food bag. Which is full of scorpions."
"They were trying to poison *her," said Li.*
"Which is why our food bag is full of scorpions?"
"And her babies."
"I feel like I shouldn't have to explain to you why our food bag should not be full of scorpions."

Artist/Creator: Vanessa Landolt
Writer: MuffinLance

● ● ● ○ ○

3/5 Chicks Confused About
Their Species

Lion Peacock

Panthera Leo Flabelliferus

The iconic lion peacock is the male with his magnificent feathered mane. Travelers to the Archival Desert would do well to keep watch for the more humbly colored peahens, who blend easily with their surroundings and hunt even the largest of prey. One notable exception to their diet is the peacock goat, the females of which lioness peahens will easily share territory with. Peahens of both species have been observed nannying the other's chicks while their mothers are away; they seem content to let their respective peacocks sort out any dominance issues. Older lioness peahens have been known to grow flamboyant manes of their own, though the reason for this is uncertain. Unlike the peacock clownfish, the changes are only external.

"If they aren't going to eat that goat, can I?" asked his human friend.

Artist/Creator: Foofymonkey
Writer: MuffinLance

5/5 I'd Like to Be
Friends-olotl

Bumbleolotl

Ambystobomba Fufysimiai

These desert pollinators have been the salvation of many
a weary traveler. Emerging at dusk, they can fly up to eight
kilometers in search of flowers, but always return to their
hive as dawn breaks. As their hives are built into the muddy
banks of ponds and rivers, thirsty travelers need only follow
the morning flight of the bumbleolotls to reach a water
source. Some colonies have existed in the same locations
for hundreds of years. As roads and landmarks can be
scarce between large settlements, bumbleolotl colonies and
flight paths form the basis of many of the most reliable
local maps.

---

*"...And they suck in pollen by creating a vacuum, and they can
regrow limbs, and—"*
"You actually like them?" asked Li.
"They're not trying to kill me."

Artist/Creator: Foofymonkey
Writer: MuffinLance

5/5 Kittenpillars in
Blankies

Luna Caracal

Papiliomanis Saltatrix

This nocturnal feline can't fly, but it can leap up to twelve
times its own height and gracefully control its descent.
It often leaves leftover prey in treetops to eat later. Mothers
will move their hatched kittenpillars to new foliage every
day and will fiercely guard them while they pupate.

"...That is a silk blanket with a kitten head sticking out."
"Mooncake is building her cocoon," said Li.

Artist/Creator: KitKatalaya
Writers: KitKatalaya and MuffinLance

9/10 Reasons to Not Stray
Off the Beaten Path

Tiger Tiger Snake

Panthera Tigris Serpentipes

Beware the camouflage of the tiger tiger snake; it can be practically invisible to its victim, blending with the shadowed wind-patterns of dunes. It can climb over 10 meters high, swim up to 30 kilometers, and hold its breath for 10 minutes or more. Thankfully it is most commonly found in the deep desert, has a solitary nature, and will display a warning before striking in anger. This aggressive predator is highly venomous, and its toxin can kill a human in hours–if they haven't been mauled to death by its fangs and claws first!

"Why don't they tell people about these things?"
"They pretty much stick to their own territory and don't like areas with a lot of humans," said Li. "Plus you really won't see or hear one unless it decides to attack. Would knowing they're out there make you feel any better?"

Artist/Creator/Writer: Delta Shout

6/10 Condors Patiently
Trailing You

Condor Giraffe

Grallator Volturius

Standing up to 5.5 meters tall, these scavengers are the bane
of Luna caracals, jewel shrike wasps, and all other predators
who thought their caches were safe up high. Their height also
allows them to see potential food from afar. Condor giraffes
can live up to sixty years. Females and their young travel in
small groups, while males form their own bachelor herds.
When a carcass is spotted, many groups may converge on
the same site. Feeding order is loosely hierarchical, with
dominance established by necking. Condor giraffes have
only two gaits: walking and galloping. They employ the
latter when faced with a serious attack from a predator, such
as lion peacocks or tiger tiger snakes. They're able to sustain
gaits of up to 50 kilometers per hour for extended periods,
but prefer an energy-conserving amble.

"Do they always follow people?"
"Only tourists," said Li.

Artist/Creator: KitKatalaya
Writers: KitKatalaya and MuffinLance

Allison M. Kovacs (MuffinLance)
Editor and Lead Writer
is a writer of SF&F short stories and novels as well as overly long fanfics. Find her on AO3, Ko-fi, Tumblr, and other sites @MuffinLance. Creator of the *Giant Isopuppy, Mimic Catopus, Polar Bear Goose,* and *Mantis Shrimp Badger.*

Titanic-Ente
Latin Name Magister and Artist
is a nerd, engineering student and hobby-artist (and a bit of a know-it-all), who draws, sculpts, paints or writes, or experiments with other creative stuff when she is in the mood. May on occasion post stuff here: www.deviant art.com/titanic-ente and more often (all those baby dragon sketches have to end up somewhere!) here: titanic-ente.tumblr.com or maybe, someday, finally here: archiveofourown.org/users/TitanicEnte

Mantis Seahorse, Mimic Catopi (contributor pages art), Pike Snail, Sweetwater Anglerfish, Vole-Bird-of-Paradise

Vanessa Landolt
Layout Editor and Artist
is a graphic designer with a passion for traveling, martial arts and chocolate, not necessarily in that order. She can be found on instagram @v_n_ss_ or on www.vanessalandolt.ch

Bat Cat, Bumblebear, Dragonfly Deer, Iguana Owl, Lionfish Weasel, Scorpion Rat

AlyssumGrey

I am a freelance artist who dreams of having my own booth at a convention. You can look me up on RedBubble under Alyssumgrey.

Owl Wolf

Bean

I like drawing, birds, and tea. You can find me on Tumblr @bean-there-done-that, and on Instagram @mean beanfightingmachine.

Anteater Snake, Crested Otter Grebe

Cally P.

is an artist and soon-to-be ecologist who thinks far too much about the biology and evolutionary history of fictional organisms. @callp on Red-bubble and Flickr.

Croc-of-the-Rock

Cara

is an avid reader, competent crocheter, and enthusiastic doodler. Someday she'll get her life together, but that day is yet to come.

Jewel Shrike Wasp

CaroloftheBell

is a lover of fanfics, and a firm believer that cuddles are the best medicine, followed closely by coffee. She has been awarded the #1 accomplice ribbon for her fan-art contributions to the muffin-verse and alleged solicitation of the genie. Despite a lack of proper artistic training she recommends fan-art to anyone who needs to cope with trauma.

Coonlion Fish, Froggull, Giant Isopuppy (title and final page art), Tiger Triceratops

celestialfeathers

is a theoretical writer and artist-which is to say that she does writing and art mostly in theory. Still, if a project is cool enough, it'll wind her up and you can just watch her go! She's planning on honing not only her crafts, but her habits around them as well. Can be found on tumblr under the name celestial-feathers.

Crow Wasp, Fairy Wrencoon

Chaotic-Energy

sometimes makes art and writes stuff, but not as regularly as she would like. Loves a lot of things and is thus always jumping from one thing to another.

Kangaroo Bird

CK

is a hobby artist who's way too into everything at once! Loves drawing, sculpting, stitchwork, and consuming massive amounts of fan content. Can be found at ckscorner.tumblr.com.

Anteater Wasp, Butterbeaver, Leafy Sea Llama, Vulture Goat

CreatureThingOE

is an artist and writer mostly pertaining to a manner of different creatures, worldbuilding, dinosaurs, trains of thought, heaps of original characters and short stories. Can be found on Tumblr @CreatureThing-OtherEntities.

Blue-Ringed Mantis Shrimproach, Drop Worm, Honeyeater Honey Possum, Killer Pteroroo, Marsupial Spinebill Mouse, Murder Moose, Pink 'n' Grey Mangabey

Deathsmallcaps

Crocodile Bumblebee, Kangaroo Dolphin, Thylacine Moa

Delta Shout

is an enthusiastic artist that dabbles in several mediums as well as fandoms. While she is currently dedicating her free time to her textile crafts, she put down the knitting needles and happily put pen to paper for this fantastic idea and amazing book.

Brush-Tailed Gecko Possum, Hopping Mouse Wren, Saltwater Crocotiel, Tiger Tiger Snake

Dragon Harris

is an artist and art teacher who enjoys making strange things. You can find her work on Instagram @dragonharris, or on Twitter @enoughdragons.

Gila Raven, Hummingbird Octopus

E. L. Perkins

is an anthropology student who likes animals and fanfic. She occasionally writes and draws, but most of her time is spent crying about cartoons and preparing for the inevitable zombie apocalypse by stalking solarpunk blogs. Can be found on tumblr at butterfly-jackal.tumblr.com (I made it specifically for this project to be honest) where she may start posting more art and stories.

Butterfly Jackal, Cobra Sandgrouse, Snapping Flamingo

Emma S.

determined to become a jack-of-all-trades, with interests ranging from crochet to geology, it isn't hard for her to find something she enjoys. However she is easily distracted by a good book, fanfiction or otherwise; much to the dismay of her many unfinished projects. She can be found on tumblr @knightowl247

Flying Kinkarten

Foofymonkey

is an artist on Tumblr who enjoys drawing strange and fun creatures and designs, leading to an abundance of OC's.
She hopes to one day write her own book and can be found on Tumblr @foofyarts.

Bumbleolotl, Lion Peacock, Vampire Bat Hummingbird

IAmTheLibrary

Just a reader, and occasionally an artist, who found this project by chance. It's the first time my art is somewhere else than in my sketchbook, which is a bit weird, but the good kind of weird.

Lamprey Pig, Maned Axolotl

J.B. MothDove

Just a guy who loves drawing, and loves other people being happy because of drawing. Enjoys reading, taking pictures, and making up stories but never being able to write them. Hopes that you have a great day! :D

Moth Dove, Seamoth

Jellybaby

A student of art history and archeology who loves making art just as much as looking at it. Does mostly traditional art but recently discovered the wonders of modern technology and now also draws digitally and occasionally dabbles in animation. Can be found on tumblr under @i-would-like-a-jellybaby or @i-would-like-some-tea where she posts fanart and all kinds of interesting/funny stuff and on instagram under the name @sunday.painter.

Blobfish Chihuahua, Great Crested Newt Beaver, Jumping Spidercat, Magpie Macaque

Jenna B

Autistic artist, geek, and teacher of children of all ages with a focus on using animals as therapy in the special needs community. In online circles just tries to be a positive light and Team Mom.

Swan Squirrel

Kaitie S

enjoys making and writing things of a fannish persuasion @InkTail on Tumblr or @Kaittzie on Twitter.

Llamion

Kendall

Kindleln has been haunted by the flying-ant-bear in her dreams, nightmares and waking life for almost a decade. Five years ago a portrait of it was almost entered into an art competition. However the world was not ready, but now it is time to unleash it upon the masses (or at least the people who bought this book). Sometimes I write, sometimes I draw @kindleln on tumblr.

Flying Ant Bear

Kibeth3

Creator of the Anteater Snake, Monarch Fox, Tiger Fish

KitKatalaya

makes art sometimes. She mostly does digital art with a focus on creature creation and the occasional fanart. Also, every once in a blue moon she writes (and even more rarely publishes). All links at linktr.ee/kitkatalaya_art.

Condor Giraffe, Fox Centipede, Gulpereel Crab, Hippo Scorpion, Lamprey Jellyfish, Long-Tailed Poison Dart Widow, Luna Caracal, Snake Urchin, Stingray Scallop, Tarantula Bat

Kristi N.

A huge fan of all things books, she dabbles in art and writing. Prefers reading, painting, and being upside down while also being a full time student! Can be found hiding in the library.

Sheep Dog

LaurJulience

Hedgehog Woodpecker, Hummingdeer, Monarch Elephant, Scorpion Frog, Spider Toucan, Turtledove

lyditist

An artist and writer in theory. Can be found on tumblr at lyditist.

Moray Eelaphant, Oyster Snake

MariDark_Art

is a traditional artist. She draws animals, fantasy and people, like creating someone new. Also often makes up stories and AUs that no one ever sees. She's spent the last 1,5 years reading AtLA fics.

Death's Head Hawkmoth Weasel (dedication page art and main entry), Dog Caiman, Hammerhead Dugong, Pheangorong, Shrike Degu

Misti_Future

is an animator/artist that loves animals, characters and amazing stories (only two of which she can actually create). She can be found @Mistical52 or @Misti-art on Tumblr and @misti_future on Instagram.

Froghog, Wolverine Molefinch

Moira H.
is an art college student whose end goal is to be a freelance artist someday, and loves figuring out how mythical animals would realistically work with what little biology she knows. First time doing anything like this, and was mostly glad just to have made the deadline but also to have been able to participate in something so fun and worthwhile!

Monarch Fox

Neko265
Simple artist that likes drawing cute stuff. Can be found on tumblr @neko265 and Twitter @Shoe_boxcat.

Fox Moth

Nicole H.
A writer of fantasy, short stories and an over abundant amount of work in progresses. Also a wanna-be artist! She can be found at forgottenfates on Tumblr and on AO3 under Panikki (warning, her fandom tastes are all over the place!)

Bush Viper Bat

Non-Plutonian Druid
is technically a paid artist, but mostly makes digital art for her own enjoyment. Her favorite things to draw include cute cats, adorable aliens, and body horror. Her store can be found on redbubble under the name Plutonian-Druid.

Hummingbird Anteater, Jellyfish Whale

Ori Kraemer
has been known to do art upon occasion. They can be found on instagram @zeesalty and on deviantArt @more-dragonstbh.

Sea Snake Lionfish

PoCATo
Novice digital artist, lover of reading and in more fandoms than is healthy, you can find me on tumblr, twitter and instagram as PoCATo, soon on patreon and kofi once I figure out how those things work.

Butterfly Raven, Moth Bat

r0-ot

Barrier Reef Dragon, Cat Fish, Ghost Seahorse, Tiger Fish

Riley
Enjoys making illustrations! Especially of weird, probably-better-that-they-don't-exist animals. You can find her on Tumblr, Instagram, and Twitter under @iiRyeBreadii.

Golden Secretary Cat, Mantis Shrimp Badger, Otter Gar, Polar Bear Goose

Shedrabbles-butitsalie

Creator of the Arctic Lobster Wolf

sheepscot
is a person who gets enthusiastic about many many art things be it writing, drawing, sewing, felting, metalsmithing, (not in that order) and so much more. Can be found on Tumblr as sheepscot and geniuspuppetmaster.

Emu Mole Rat, Peacock Goat

SnazzyAddie

Goldjaw

stardumb
A little freelance artist with big dreams of someday going pro. An aspiring animator and concept artist with a penchant for the macabre, she can be frequently found in her natural habitats of coffee shops and probably haunted libraries honing her craft. Will bury you in about a million pictures of her rabbits if you let her. Art can be found @ stardumb.tumblr.com

Frobbit, Mimic Catopus (main entry), Owl Spider

Stydealized
is an artist and occasional writer who loves far too many fandoms all at once. They love worldbuilding and has way too many AUs and projects in the works. (Seriously, WAY too many.) Find them on Youtube, Deviantart and Tumblr under the same names!

Parrot Hyena

ThimbleHouses
is an art student; working mostly in mixed media illustration. You can find her on Tumblr @Thimblehouses or Instagram @Thimblehouse.

Emperor Tortoise Moth

ThisCat
Nearly finished with her programming bachelors, ThisCat writes and draws as a way to relax.

Harekat, Serpentfly

Timx
is an artist that writes on occasion. A lover of animated shows and fantasy stories, they only lurk on tumblr at timxstuff where they will occasionally remember to post their art.

Giant Isopuppy (main entry)

WhisperWolf
is the winner of the cover coloring contest.

How to get your free PDF

Bought the physical book?
Send your order number to LisBookOfFriends@gmail.com
with "Book PDF" in the subject line.

Got the book as a gift?
Color your favorite picture, slap a "today's date" sticky
note on it, and send the photo as above.

Reading this in someone else's copy and want your own?
Donate 10 USD or more to WIRES (wires.org.au)
and forward the donation confirmation email to LisBook
OfFriends@gmail.com with "Donation PDF" in the
subject line.

**Obtained the PDF version already through Totally
Legal Means**[Oops Not Really] **and are feeling the slowburn guilt
of taking money from a charity?**
Donate as above when you're financially able and be absolved
of your coloring book sins.